FLAMES OF HATE

JAY NADAL

Published by 282publishing.com

1

NATASHA PUSHED her head back into the headrest and closed her eyes for a few moments as Marcus drove back to their bed-and-breakfast. Her mind drifted back to the romantic evening they had just shared at Lowry Eight, a local dining hotspot known for using local, farm-fresh ingredients. Her thoughtful husband had planned the ideal weekend away for them to celebrate their first wedding anniversary, keeping everything a secret until the last minute.

She smiled and opened her eyes before staring ahead into the inky blackness, the road barely lit in the headlights, neither of them in a hurry to get back to the bed-and-breakfast, even though it was one a.m. With her windows down, the lingering heat of the warm summer night still bathed her face.

She took a deep breath in and savoured the clean fresh air that filled her lungs. Perhaps it was the mix of the atmosphere, the wine, and being away from home. She felt giddy, but in a good way. The wind whipped through her hair, fanning it over the headrest. Natasha reached across and squeezed her husband's thigh and smiled at him. Placing one hand on Natasha's, he squeezed in return, never taking his eyes off the road.

Words seemed unnecessary since both were at ease with the silence and the stillness that surrounded them. Natasha wasn't even sure where they were. The long, dark, winding road seemed to go on forever, and tall hedgerows masked her view of the surrounding landscape. So far, the trip had been perfect. She'd cooed with surprise when they'd first arrived at the isolated farm, almost not believing that Marcus had found such a beautiful place. The dinner was gorgeous and romantic, with Marcus arranging for flowers to be waiting for them at the table.

"It would be so lovely to live up here, wouldn't it?"

Marcus laughed. "Give it a month, and you'd be bored. You'd miss your friends too much and your Friday night out with the girls."

Marcus had a point, but she continued to face this internal struggle between enjoying a busy social life and yearning to be surrounded by rolling hills and clean, crisp air.

"Yeah, I know you're right. But it doesn't stop me from dreaming about it. What a lovely place to grow up. Can you imagine if we moved out here as a family?" she mused.

Marcus laughed. "Give us a chance. We've only been married a year and now you're talking about relocating us as a couple to the middle of nowhere."

Natasha suppressed a laugh. Marcus had always been anti-countryside. He loved the big city, the bright lights, the honking taxis, busy buses, and congested platforms on the

London Underground. For him to bring her to the middle of nowhere only showed her just how much he loved her. Natasha made a promise to herself that she would make it up to him when they got back to their accommodation. The wine had been free-flowing, the food amazing, and the company... Well, she couldn't think of anyone else she would rather spend her time with. Though her mum came a close second.

"We must grab a bit of their farm produce before heading home. Mum would love some of their cheese," Natasha commented.

"Yes, that sounds like a good idea. They seem to do a good range."

Marcus narrowed his eyes at a glimmer of light in front of him. The light was moving, which confirmed an approaching car from the opposite direction. Marcus gripped the wheel, knowing that it would be a tight squeeze along a single narrow lane.

"Look out," Natasha screamed as she grabbed the handle on her door and thrust her hand out towards the dash to brace herself.

Marcus gasped as a bright set of headlights loomed into view and headed straight towards them.

"They're not slowing down!" Natasha screamed.

Marcus jammed his foot on the brake and pulled his wheel to the left, forcing his car into the hedgerow as his tyres screeched along the road. The speeding vehicle left the scene in an instant, whizzing past, not stopping, rocking their car in its wake as its rear lights disappeared.

"Bloody locals," Marcus fumed. "They've got no consideration for others. Yes, fair enough they know these roads like the back of their hand, but if our car had been any wider, we wouldn't have been able to avoid a head-on collision."

Natasha threw a hand over her face as her heart pounded in her chest. They had been seconds and inches away from a serious accident. She dreaded to imagine what would have happened if Marcus hadn't been able to pull over and come to a stop. "Do you think we've damaged the car?" Natasha asked, blowing her cheeks.

In all the commotion, neither of them had paid attention to the scraping noise that lasted a few seconds as the car came to a halt alongside one of the overgrown hedgerows.

"I think we scraped the side of the car. Bastard. I'll have to have a look at it properly tomorrow morning. Hopefully, I can get most of the scratches out with T-Cut. The main thing is that we're both safe and there's no further damage to the car. It could easily have been a lot worse than that. As he came barrelling towards us, I had visions of us rolling into a ditch and ending up on our roof."

Natasha glanced across at Marcus. "Don't say that."

Marcus started the car and pulled off again, driving slower this time as he took one bend after another, his eyes darting and searching into the darkness for any signs of other approaching vehicles.

As they neared the bed-and-breakfast, Natasha noticed the sky ahead of them beginning to lighten. The golden glow was in marked contrast to the inky blackness of the surrounding sky.

"Looks like the farmer has a fire going," she observed. "A bit late for that?"

Marcus shrugged. "Perhaps it's the best time to do it. It's cooler than it has been during the day. Maybe it's easier for him to control."

Natasha shrugged as they got closer. As Marcus steered the car through the last bend, she gasped. Up ahead of them as the hedgerow cleared, she saw the farmhouse across the road from the bed-and-breakfast engulfed in fire, the orange and yellow flames pirouetting and dancing to their own tune against a blackened backdrop.

Marcus approached the farmhouse and pulled in through the gates, only to see the real horror unfolding in front of them. The whole farmhouse was ablaze. He reached for his phone and dialled 999 before jumping out of the car.

"Marcus!" Natasha shouted through the open driver's door. "It's too dangerous. Don't get too close."

"There must be people in there. I need to help," he replied.

Natasha threw open her door and raced around to his side, grabbing hold of his arm to stop him from going any further. The heat from the fire warmed their faces and prickled their skin. The intense heat was so overpowering they both took a few steps back.

Natasha's hand tightened around Marcus's arm as she screamed. "Look!" she shouted, jabbing a finger towards the first floor of the farmhouse.

Marcus glanced up and, for a brief second, there appeared to be a person banging their fists against the window before they disappeared in an orange glow.

2

As DCI KAREN HEATH pulled off the main road and turned into the large expanse of courtyard that framed the front of the farmhouse, she yawned and looked through the windscreen. It was four a.m., sunrise was still three hours away, but the darkness was dissolving around her. Outside, several ambulances, three fire engines, and half a dozen police cars were scattered across the forecourt. Officers stood in small huddles, exchanging notes, and watching the fire service tackle pockets of fire. Karen glanced around and noticed that they had set up a perimeter around the property with all fire personnel within the contained area. The remaining emergency service staff held back beyond the cordon.

Karen yawned again and took a deep breath before stepping out and locking the car behind her. She made her way towards the taped cordon, her sleepy mind challenging her to take in the scene. From what she could tell, it was an isolated farmhouse, and other than the adjoining outbuildings, which she imagined belonged to this property, there were no other dwellings. No pockets of light, no passing vehicles, just an emptiness that cocooned them. In front of her, residual heat from the fire warmed the air. She sniffed and then wished she had brought her wellies with her. *When will I learn?*

Pinching her nose, she looked at the ground. Cowpats everywhere. With the acrid smell of fire combining with the smell of slurry and shit, bile scorched her throat. *Terrific.* "Move to York. It will be great. A fresh start. Lots of challenging cases. No one mentioned the bloody cow shit everywhere," she muttered beneath her breath.

Karen scanned the yard and looked on as firemen dressed in breathing apparatus came in and out of the building. Their red hoses criss-crossed each other as they snaked from various fire engines. Two hoses disappeared through the front door, whilst they trained the third on the upstairs windows where the glass had blown out from the heat. Swirling black smoke spewed from the openings. It was as if the smoke was desperate to escape the confines of the building.

Karen joined her uniformed colleague. "What have we got?"

"Ma'am. We were called out a few hours ago. By the time we got here, the fire had already taken hold. The fire service are still trying to tackle deep-seated pockets of it," he said, nodding towards the building. "They are also dealing with hazardous substances. Hypochlorite, or something like that. That all needs to be made safe before we can get in there."

"Were the family inside?" Karen asked, stuffing her hands in her pockets as she looked on, her mind racing.

"The farm is owned by the Lawsons. We've carried out a quick search of the surrounding area and we've not discovered any casualties."

Karen nodded, understanding the seriousness of the situation. "Are they in there?"

"Yes, ma'am." The officer took in a deep breath and then coughed as the acrid smell tickled the back of his throat. "It looks like the whole family didn't make it out. Three generations, I believe. Old man Lawson. A retired farmer. His son took over the farm. Runs it with his wife and three grown-up kids."

"Shit."

"I spoke to one lad from the fire service. He said it's bloody grim in there."

It wasn't the news Karen wanted to hear. House fires were always difficult scenes to witness. Luckily, the ones that she had attended in London hadn't all been as bad as this. She had attended a few where the occupants had perished in the flames. The images of the charred bodies would stay with her until her last breath. The prospect of going in there didn't sit comfortably with her.

"Who called it in?"

The officer thumbed back over his shoulder. "Marcus and Natasha Sutton. They're renting a B & B across the road. It's also owned by the Lawsons. There were coming back from a night out when they saw the place up in flames. There was nothing they could do."

"Anyone looking after them?"

The officer nodded. "A PCSO is with them. The paramedics have given them the once-over to make sure they're okay. Other than being in shock, they're coping."

"Okay, thanks." Karen walked away from the officer and followed the line of the cordon tape until she had a clearer view of the side of the building. The devastation that met her concerned gaze wasn't much better than the front. Nearly every window had been blown out. A few from the flames, others would have been from the fire service. They had set up arc lights to illuminate the darkness. She imagined the farmhouse was once a nice-looking, traditional building, but in its current state it was hardly recognisable. Black smoke stained the whitewashed walls. Once a happy family home, she suspected it would soon be condemned for demolition once the fire had done its work.

Her shoulders sagged as Karen stood alone away from everyone else. Nausea and sadness weighed her down in equal measure. It was bad enough standing out here, her mind in a mixture of turmoil and grief. But she needed to psych herself up for what she would discover once inside.

3

KAREN CHECKED the time on her phone. Four thirty a.m. She'd only been here thirty minutes, but it felt more like a few hours. Semi-darkness still surrounded them. People were still asleep in their beds, but the scene that played out in front of her was a hive of activity. Fire service personnel busied themselves as they continued to bring the fire under control. She noticed two firemen donning hazmat suits before disappearing towards an adjoining building, dragging a red hose across the yard.

The station officer was barking commands at his team, whilst another officer with a large whiteboard stood back speaking into his radio. Karen couldn't hear his words, but she imagined he was keeping track of everyone on the whiteboard and ticking off their locations as well as how much air time remained in the BA kits before they needed to be replaced with a fresh crew. Another fire appliance swung in through the gates and parked up away from the property before another crew jumped out to help where necessary.

The heat from the fire was intense. Karen felt her cheeks reddening again as she moved closer towards the perimeter tape, which kept everyone safe and away from the main building. With a fire this powerful, there was always the risk of exploding glass, a timber roof collapsing and potential gas explosions from ruptured gas lines. There was the added concern and risk of it being an industrial place of work, which meant chemical fertilisers, cleaning products, as well as on some farms, methane storage tanks.

Karen ran a hand through her hair. Other members of her team would arrive soon. She'd called through to the station on her way to the scene, asking the night shift to get a few bodies out of bed.

"Ma'am."

An approaching officer jolted Karen from her thoughts. She turned to see a uniformed colleague in a hi-vis jacket marching towards her.

"Yep," Karen replied.

"We've got a lady by the main gate. Her name is Ellen, and she helps on the farm with milking the cows. She wants a word with the person in charge."

Karen offered the smallest of nods. "Okay, lead the way," Karen said as she pulled a face and stared at the ground, watching where she placed her feet, realising that the cowpats that she had seen on arrival had now been squashed into the concrete floor or mixed with the water being used to douse the flames. She was thankful she couldn't smell them, the heady aroma of burning wood masking the scent.

Karen stopped by the gate to find a woman that looked to be in her mid-thirties, standing there with arms folded across her chest. The woman's hair reminded Karen of a poorly constructed bird's nest, scrawny and untidy with bits sticking out. She wore a thick outdoor waxy jacket, dark leggings and wellington boots.

"I'm Detective Chief Inspector Karen Heath from York police. I understand you wanted a word with the person in charge. Well, here I am. You are?"

Ellen cleared her throat. "I'm Ellen Turner, the herd person. I deal with the cows and the milking process on John's farm as well as on other local farms where they need extra help. What's bloody happened?"

"And John is?"

Ellen stood rooted to the spot. Her eyes fixed on the burning farmhouse, the flickering flames that tumbled from the windows reflected in the whites of her eyes.

Karen repeated the question.

Ellen cleared her throat again. "Um. John. John Lawson. He owns the farm. I'm always here after four a.m. to get the herd milked before sending them back out for the day to graze."

"Well, as you can see, we've got our hands full at the moment. I'll need to speak to you at some point. But our primary concern is bringing the fire under control as well as discovering what happened to the occupants."

Ellen's eyes widened. She jabbed a finger towards the farmhouse. "You mean. You mean… you don't know where they are? Are you telling me they're in there?" Her tone was one of concern and shock as she gasped.

"We are not sure at the moment. The fire service is trying to bring the fire under control whilst searching the property. We've not discovered any of the occupants in the surrounding area, so I think you need to prepare for the worst."

Ellen staggered back a few steps before grabbing hold of the gate to steady herself.

Karen stepped forward and grabbed Ellen's arm. "Are you okay? Do you need to sit down?"

Ellen shook her head. "No. No... I'll be fine. It's just come as a shock. I don't think they're away. John would have told me, as it would have meant extra work here. That must mean that they are in..."

"We'll know shortly," Karen replied softly. "I've spoken to an officer from the rural policing team who told me it was the Lawson farm. But he couldn't confirm how many occupants it had. I imagine you would know if you were here daily?"

"Yes. There are six of them. John and his wife Andrea who run the farm. Then there's John's dad, William, but he's older and retired. Confined to a wheelchair for most of his time. John has three kids. Matthew, Jessica, and Robert. All grown-up."

"And all six live here permanently?" Karen asked.

"Yes. Matt, Jess and Robert all help on the farm. How come no one got out when the fire started?"

Karen didn't have an answer for that and could only shrug in reply. That was a question she had asked herself several times since arriving.

"I'm gonna have to do something with the cattle. Their udders are going to be painful if someone doesn't milk them soon."

As if on cue, the cattle in the adjoining field jostled and pushed by the gate, the clasp rattling as they leant into it. It was as if they had heard Ellen's voice. They mooed, grunted, snorted and bellowed their displeasure.

Karen looked around. There was no way she could allow the woman in. Ellen had already pointed out that the milking parlour was on the other side of the courtyard which would entail her ushering the herd right past the farmhouse, emergency service vehicles and the many hoses that snaked their way from the appliances to the farmhouse.

"This is an active scene. You will not be able to milk them here."

"That's what I thought you would say," Ellen replied as she zipped up her jacket. "I'll take the herd across the field and move them to the farm across the back. The Wagstaff farm. They won't mind. They have plenty of land. I can get them milked there."

Just as Karen was finishing her conversation with Ellen and taking the woman's number, the trumpeting of an air horn made her jump. She glanced over her shoulder to see a large milk tanker arriving. "Bloody hell! I nearly jumped out of my skin."

"Yep. It's enough to wake the dead," Ellen replied, glancing back towards the farmhouse and realising what she had said. "I'll speak to the tanker driver. He's here to pick up the milk from the Lawsons. I'll divert him to the Wagstaffs."

"Okay, thanks. I'll be in touch, Ellen. Thanks for your time." Karen turned and headed back towards the scene.

4

"ANY CHANCE I can get in there now?" Karen asked, a hint of frustration creeping into her voice. She'd been at the scene for five hours. By nine a.m., the fire had been put out, and any residual pockets of heat dampened down. Having been informed that the remains of six occupants had been discovered, the situation had taken on a more serious element.

Fire Incident Commander Carlo Jenrick removed his helmet and ruffled his brown, sweaty hair before blowing out his cheeks.

He'd arrived a few hours earlier to oversee the scene and coordinate the response by the fire service. Karen hadn't met him before today, and her impressions of him had been favourable when he had first introduced himself a few hours ago. She put him in his late forties, with a slim face that matched his thin frame. Though he said little, he carried an air of leadership about him. The few words he did say elicited an immediate response whenever he spoke to one of his team. The man hadn't barked once, but whenever he needed something done, she noticed him placing a hand on the shoulder of whoever he was talking to and laying out his instructions in a soft and measured tone.

Though he'd been at the scene for as many hours, he looked bright and alert with a visible softness to his smile that reached his eyes. She wondered if he had kids and whether he spoke to them in much the same way. Soft, reassuring, and direct with a hint of assertiveness.

He offered Karen a smile. "You've been incredibly patient. Structurally, the building is unsafe for you to wander around on your own. We're still assessing the damage, but I can certainly accompany you."

"Works for me. My team will arrive any second, so I want to grab a first impression before I talk to them."

"Follow me. Let's get you kitted up with gloves and a face mask."

Karen fell in line behind him as they headed over towards a nearby appliance, where Jenrick rolled up one shutter and pulled out the equipment. Having waited a few moments for Karen to don the gloves and mask, he led her to the front door. He paused by the entrance and glanced towards Karen.

"I'll warn you now. It smells a bit in here. If you thought the acrid smell was bad out there, wait until you get inside." Jenrick paused. "The victims are upstairs. I've had a look. Not pretty."

Karen nodded. "Thanks for the heads-up. I've attended a few house fires before, so I think I'll be okay."

Jenrick nodded as he disappeared into the darkened doorway, followed swiftly by Karen. The intense heat hit Karen

first, a suffocating, warm, choking temperature that smoth-
ered her. She was thankful for the mask, as warm air filled
her lungs. She followed Jenrick through the darkened hallway. Paint blistered on the woodwork and blackened soot
trails snaked down the walls. Her feet squelched in the slippery puddles that collected on the flagstone floors. Karen
carefully stepped over wet, sticky ash and broken timber.

Karen followed Jenrick around the ground floor of the
farmhouse. It was an appalling scene. Grey smoke hung in
the stillness of each room. Small pockets of steam escaped
from the now burnt furnishings, the smoke trails pirouetting up to meet the grey clouds. Each room they entered
showed the violent path that the raging fire had taken,
destroying everything in its way. Karen stopped in what she
presumed was once the dining room. The blackened
remains of a dining table and half a dozen chairs lay in a
broken mess as if a tornado had just whipped through the
room.

Until now, Jenrick had remained silent, allowing Karen to
be with her thoughts as she assessed the scene. He stopped
and stepped to one side of the dining room. "A fair few
bottles are littered around here, mainly confined to this
room."

Karen nodded. Most were coated in a layer of black soot. A
few, like the windows, had exploded in the heat. *Wine
bottles*. She counted seven intact, and another three or four
which had exploded.

"You ready for the rest of it?" Jenrick asked, flicking his
eyes towards the ceiling.

"I don't think we're ever ready for it."

Karen followed Jenrick up the stairs, taking each tread carefully after he warned her that fire damage would have weakened the staircase.

With less smoke upstairs, Jenrick mentioned that Karen would be okay for a few minutes to take off her face mask. When she did without hesitation, a noxious smell hit her. A familiar smell. Once experienced, never forgotten. Burnt flesh.

Jenrick guided her into the nearest bedroom. The scene took her breath away as her steps faltered. The charred remains of two bodies lay on a double bed. It was hard for Karen to decide who they were or even what sex they were. Their flesh had been left bubbled and boiled into a black, charred and sticky mess.

"Jesus. That's so fucking tragic."

"You okay?" Jenrick asked.

Karen shook her head. There were no words to describe the horrific sight. Having observed enough, Karen left the room and inspected the other rooms. Three bedrooms, one twisted and charred body in each. The scene in the last one nearly broke Karen. She stood alongside Jenrick, their shoulders almost touching. Though she didn't want to admit it, she needed to stand close to him in case it all became too much. A sheen of sweat broke out across her brow, and a sliver of fear prickled her skin as her mind tumbled through the graphic images flashing through her thoughts. Screaming voices. Terrified eyes. Panic. Scorching burns. *How much did they suffer?* she wondered.

A flash of metal caught her eye and her stomach plummeted. But the twisted metal in the middle of the room didn't upset her the most. It was the charred remains of a body lying beside it that left her speechless. Almost curled up into an embryonic form, Grandad Lawson had tried to escape in the final few moments of his life. Knees tucked into his chest, one arm outstretched close to the wheelchair, blackened fingers wrapped around a piece of the frame, melted by the heat and fixed in place for everyone to see.

Three generations. Their lives extinguished in a matter of minutes.

Karen blinked hard and wiped away a tear with the back of her glove. She wasn't sure if it was from seeing the bodies or from the residual heat and smell creeping into her lungs. A nagging question took root in Karen's mind. *Were they murdered first and then the farmhouse set alight to destroy the evidence, or did they die as the fire took hold?*

5

DEEP IN THOUGHT, Karen paced up and down the courtyard. With her arms folded across her chest, and her head down, she needed the space to think things through. It also gave her the opportunity to clear her head, but that was proving a challenge. The pictures of the charred remains of the Lawson family punctured her thoughts. For the time being she had to assume their identities until they could be confirmed.

The noises continued behind her. The sound of generators on board the fire engines whirred in the background. A dozen conversations echoed around her as fire service personnel ran through the checklist of what needed to be done to contain and secure the building. The ambulances had long since gone, their services not needed, and Karen now waited for the private ambulances that would take the bodies away.

"Bloody hell," came a voice behind her.

Karen turned to see Jade and Ty stepping through the puddles whilst at the same time throwing looks towards the farmhouse as they took in the scene.

"It certainly is, Jade," Karen replied with a deep sigh.

"You said it was bad, but I wasn't expecting this."

The three of them stood still for a moment and looked up at the farmhouse. Its smart and rustic white façade had been replaced by blackened trails of soot, and fire damage. The intense heat had crumbled the plaster and punctured the tiled roof that had probably been there for decades. Gaping holes showed the charred timber remains of roof struts, which now resembled a bony ribcage.

Ty blew out a whistle through his lips. "Do we have a cause for the fire?"

Karen shook her head. "Not at the moment. The fire investigator is in there now. Janet Reed. I spoke with her briefly. Are you familiar with her, Ty?"

"Nope. Not heard of her. But then again, I've not been called out to many house fires."

"Anything you want us to do?" Jade asked.

"I don't think there is much we can do until we can get back in there again. Ideally, I wanted you to see the remains of the occupants in situ. Not a pleasant job, but it needed to be done. But the fire incident commander informed me that the structure is a little unsafe for us to walk around on our own."

Jade grimaced. "Was it that bad?"

Karen nodded as she stared towards the farmhouse. Her silence was enough.

"Any witnesses?" Jade asked, looking around the courtyard and surrounding farm buildings.

"Not as far as I can gather. It's not overlooked by anyone, and there isn't a lot of passing traffic either. The nearest farm is just up the road." Karen updated Jade and Ty about her conversation with Ellen, the herdsperson, and how the herd needed milking up at the Wagstaff farm.

Karen asked Jade and Ty to stay at the scene whilst she went over to speak with Marcus and Natasha. After crossing the small narrow lane, she headed through another farm gate into a large courtyard where three small barns had been converted into boutique bed-and-breakfast apartments. Each one looked stylish from the front, featuring dark panelled wood and black window frames. *I bet this cost a few bob*, she thought as she made her way towards the only barn that had a car parked outside—a small black Astra.

Karen pushed open the door to find Diane, a PCSO that she had seen before, lurking in the first doorway off the hall. As Karen approached, the female officer looked over her shoulder and nodded. Diane stepped forward.

"How are they coping?" Karen asked in a whispered tone.

"They're doing okay considering what they've seen. Natasha was pretty shaken up to begin with, but I've made them both a cup of strong sweet tea and spoken to them at length. I think she's calmed down now."

"Okay, thanks."

"Ma'am, do you mind if I step out for a bit? I need some fresh air."

"Of course. No problem. Thanks for sitting with them. I need to ask a few questions. Is someone coming to relieve you?"

"I'm going to radio the station. My shift finished a couple of hours ago and I think they've forgotten about me."

"Crikey, Diane. I'm sorry about that. You should have been relieved sooner. Tell them to get someone here ASAP. If they give you any shit, let me know and I'll chase it up for you."

Diane shot her a grateful look. "Thanks, ma'am."

With Diane heading off, Karen made her way into the first room which appeared to be the lounge, a large spacious area, with tall ceilings, exposed beams, flagstone floors, and a sense of airiness as light flooded in from dual aspect floor-to-ceiling windows.

Marcus and Natasha were sitting huddled close together on one sofa holding hands. Karen noticed the look of concern on their faces as she walked in and introduced herself.

"I'm Detective Chief Inspector Karen Heath from York police. I'm overseeing the police response to the house fire across the road. I'm sorry we have kept you waiting, but as you can imagine, it's hectic over there."

Marcus shook his head. "That's… that's okay. I know you have a job to do, and I'm sorry we couldn't help. We felt helpless standing outside, but we didn't know what to do."

Karen held out her hand to reassure Marcus. "It's absolutely fine. You did the right thing. You called 999. In a situation like that, we wouldn't advise anyone to go into a burning building. It's too dangerous."

Marcus looked across to his wife, before returning his gaze to Karen. "I understand there were people inside. Were they… rescued?"

Karen didn't want to break the bad news to them, so needed to move them off the subject quickly. "We've got fire officers in there now searching for the occupants. Can you tell me what happened in the run-up to you making the call?"

It took a few moments for Marcus to compose himself until he could tell Karen about their evening out and their journey home. He explained how they had nearly been run off the road by a speeding motorist coming in the opposite direction moments before they'd approached the farmhouse.

Karen interrupted. "Could you make out the vehicle? The colour, make, model?"

Marcus blew out his cheeks and looked across to Natasha, who gave Karen an apologetic shrug.

"I'm sorry, no. It all happened so quickly that it took us by surprise," Marcus added.

Karen checked her notes for a few moments before continuing. "You told one of my officers that you think you may have seen someone in an upstairs window."

Marcus glanced at his wife. "I didn't see anything, but Natasha thinks she saw something."

"Natasha?" Karen asked.

Natasha sighed and chewed on her bottom lip as she wrung her hands in a tight ball in her lap. "I think I did. I think I saw hands bang against the window, and then they disappeared. It was over in a matter of seconds."

"Male? Female? Did you see a face?" Karen probed.

Natasha shrugged and closed her eyes for a few moments before opening them. "Just hands. Maybe they were trying to escape or attract attention." Natasha's voice trailed off as she looked at the floor.

Karen stood and tucked her notepad into her jacket. "Okay, thanks for that. We've got your contact details. You're free to go. I'm really sorry that you had such an awful ending to your anniversary."

Karen left them to pack away their belongings as she headed out across the track back towards the farmhouse. A farm shop on the road to her right caught her attention. It had an impressive frontage and backed out on to the far corner of the courtyard to the farmhouse. An array of rosettes and framed awards hung in one window. She made a mental note to check it out later.

6

THE FIRE INVESTIGATOR stood near the front door as Karen approached. In her late thirties, Janet had a thin frame, a round face, and blonde hair tied tight into a ponytail that she tucked inside her white paper suit.

"Janet, how are you getting on?" Karen asked as she paused near the doorway. In Karen's eyes, it was essential to have the scene exhaustively investigated especially if their examination uncovered an arson that had resulted in the tragic death of six occupants.

"Pretty good, actually. But it's also quite challenging. It's impossible to preserve the scene and evidence once a fire takes hold. Not only will a fire like this rage with such intensity," Janet said, nodding towards the building, "and destroy physical proof, but the water and any chemical foam used to put out the blaze can destroy potential evidence. So, it makes my job a real ball-ache sometimes. I've taken the time to speak to the firefighters who first arrived on the scene. They are our best witnesses."

Karen furrowed her brow, not sure what Janet was getting at.

Spotting that, Janet continued. "Sorry, let me explain. The firefighters can give us a lot of information that can help us find what may have been used to start the fire. Such as the colour of the smoke, the condition of doors and windows, and the general strange behaviour of the flames. That helps me to look for a point of origin and any other physical evidence that I can note. All of that can help me reconstruct the event and use scientific methods to find the cause of the fire."

"Do you think it was arson?" Karen asked.

Janet's brows pulled together. "In one word, yes."

The news gave Karen a whole fresh new perspective. This wasn't the tragic case of someone leaving a cigarette burning on a couch, or a chip pan fire that got out of control, or a candle on a windowsill that set the curtains alight. She had attended house fires with all of those causes during her career. Arson was something else entirely. Having dealt with those cases as well, she knew the motives behind arson were often linked to vandalism, thrill-seeking, concealment of a crime, insurance scams, revenge, and even mental illness. What she needed to figure out was which one applied in this situation.

Karen titled her head to the side. "What did you find?"

Janet referred to her notes to substantiate her assessment. "For starters, a large amount of damage. I couldn't find a 'V' burn pattern or high heat stress. I ruled out any accidental causes. Having spoken to the firefighters as well, they observed that the fire wasn't acting normally, and the colour of the smoke suggested the use of accelerants."

Karen jotted down her own notes as she listened to Janet's feedback. The evidence raised more questions than answers in Karen's mind. Someone had deliberately set out to either harm the Lawsons or their property.

"With arson, there can often be multiple points of origin, but I only found one. The front door and back doors were both locked from the inside, the keys still in the locks. But a side door was unlocked, and I believe this was the point of entry."

Karen nodded with interest. "All the windows locked as well?"

"The downstairs ones were," Janet replied and checked her notes before continuing. "All the upstairs windows were unlocked. You have to wonder why they didn't try to escape unless they were overcome by the fire quickly."

"One of our witnesses said she thought she might have seen hands at one window upstairs. Perhaps banging on the glass. Any evidence of that?"

"I noticed trails in the smoke damage to the glass in the upstairs bedroom," Janet said, pointing up towards one window to the front of the property. "Fingers could make them, but there are other marks thinner than that. Perhaps nails?"

Karen listened as Janet finished her assessment before thanking her.

Izzy Armitage, the pathologist, and Bart Lynch, the CSI manager, joined Karen moments later. They had both lingered for the last hour waiting to get in, but Jenrick, the fire incident commander, was being a stickler for the rules and had stopped them from gaining access.

"This is getting bloody ridiculous," Izzy hissed. "Doesn't that imbecile know I need to get in there? Anyone would think I haven't got a job to go to."

Karen rubbed Izzy's back. "I know. It's frustrating. But I can't afford to have you or Bart going in there and then the bloody roof collapsing on you. As soon as Jenrick is happy that they have stabilised the place, he will let you in. His boys are in there at the moment, taking down any ceiling boards that have been damaged."

"That's not what we need," Bart interjected. "They could drop those boards on vital evidence."

Karen shrugged. It was a catch-22 situation. Preserving the scene versus making the scene safe. No one was going to come out a winner. "Bart, can you and your team do the forensics outside? The fire investigator informed me that the point of entry was a side door, and she believes that's where the fire started. We can at least get your team working on that."

Bart rolled his eyes in submission before reaching down to grab his bag. "It will have to do. But promise me you'll give me a shout the second we're allowed in?"

"I promise. Now bugger off and get out of my hair."

"I really need to get in there, Karen," Izzy repeated, pacing round in a small circle. "I can't really do my work standing out here, can I? I'll get on with paperwork in my car, and you can give me a shout when you get the all-clear?"

"Yep, let's do that. I'm sorry that you had to wait around. But this is tricky. As soon as I know anything, I'll give you a shout." Karen checked her phone. It was two p.m. She had been on the scene for ten hours.

Alone again, Karen took a moment to scan all the buildings. She spotted CCTV cameras, but none were pointing in her direction or towards the farmhouse. There were three she could see overlooking the hay barns, tractor and cattle sheds. *There have to be more*, she thought, as she set off to see whether or not she was right.

7

Frustrated with her search, Karen paused in front of one of the hay barns and rested her hands on her hips. Her search of the immediate buildings hadn't resulted in finding any further cameras. Karen had been certain she would have discovered more.

Spotting Karen's perplexed look, Ty navigated the smelly, messy courtyard and made his way towards her. "Everything okay, Karen?"

"I'm not sure." Karen scrunched her eyes before rubbing them with the heels of her hands. "For a start, I'm bloody knackered. And second, there must be thousands of pounds of equipment here, but the Lawsons had three piddly little CCTV cameras. Why wouldn't they have more?"

Ty offered nothing more than a shrug. "Could have been removed? Maybe there's not a lot of theft around here?"

Karen shook her head. "Completely the opposite from what I can gather. Having liaised with the rural farming team, theft of red fuel, diggers, quad bikes, and other large items, is rife. Apparently, farmers are blocking entrances to fields with old hay trolleys, fallen trees, and concrete blocks. They're doing anything to stop people from getting on their land and nicking stuff."

Turning towards the barns, she held out her hands, palms up. "I mean, look at this kit. A Massey Ferguson tractor, a Ford tractor, a compact tractor kind of thing," Karen said with a shrug, "a trailer box, another long wheel bed trailer with ramps… They must cost a few bob?"

Tyler nodded. "A second-hand tractor is about twelve grand. Trailers are a grand or two, but I can't be certain."

"Exactly. There must be at least twenty grand worth of machinery here. Surely, you'd be watching this like a hawk? And if you had CCTV trained on this stuff, why would you not have CCTV in the courtyard in case a couple of scroats turned up and nicked one of these things?"

"Perhaps a security lapse on their part," Ty replied as he followed Karen, who'd wandered off to scope the rest of the immediate area. "Karen, I've spoken to Bart. He can't pick up any footprints from the courtyard. There are too many, and most of those belong to the emergency services. There are impressions in the cowpats, but…" Ty shrugged one shoulder.

"You're saying Bart isn't very hopeful of picking up solid forensic evidence for us."

"Pretty much," Ty replied.

"We know the Wagstaff farm is close. Can you find out what other farms are in the vicinity? Start within a one-mile radius, and if that doesn't throw up much, extend the radius in mile increments up to five miles to begin with."

Ty nodded. "Will do, Karen. Anything else?"

"No. If you can manage that for me, that would be enormously helpful. I'm going to organise a search team to scan the immediate area and surrounding fields. I want to see if we can find anything of interest like discarded accelerant bottles or cans, clothing left behind, maybe even a torn fragment of clothing snagged on that," Karen said, pointing towards a tall hedgerow that extended along the boundary of the garden behind the farmhouse.

Karen and Ty continued walking through a field as they made their way up a shallow incline until they reached the brow of the hill. The elevated position gave Karen a much clearer view of the farm and its layout. A smoky haze hovered above the farmhouse as if a pocket of fog hadn't been lifted or blown away.

The warm afternoon sun bathed her face. It felt peaceful where she stood, and a far cry from what had happened a few hundred yards down the hill. She glanced over her shoulder and saw nothing but peaceful, rolling green hills, each one bordered from its adjoining neighbour by a natural barrier made of shrubs and trees such as hawthorn, blackthorn, hazel and ash. A rich and diverse habitat for nesting birds, insects and small mammals. It was a strange juxtaposition that she found herself in.

Karen caught up with Ty, who had continued to walk around the edge of the field before making his way back towards the farmhouse. It was fast approaching six p.m. by the time Karen returned. The fire engines had gone, leaving a gaping hole in the courtyard which had seemed so congested just a few hours ago. A small catering van had arrived, and officers had formed an orderly queue to grab refreshments and a quick bite to eat. Due to the remote location, many couldn't return to the station for their rest breaks, so the arrival of the van provided a welcome relief.

Janet Reed, the fire investigator, made her way over to Karen. "You should grab yourself a sandwich and a cup of tea. You've been here all day. You must be knackered."

Karen nodded wearily. "And hungry. I'll get something in a second. I'll let the rest of the crew get their grub first."

Janet laughed. "I thought you'd pull rank and push to the front of the queue."

Karen looked over towards the queue again and narrowed her eyes. "Oh, trust me. The thought had crossed my mind, but I can't be arsed."

Janet pulled the red scrunchie from her long blonde ponytail and unzipped her white paper suit overalls. "I've given Bart and his team the go-ahead to begin their internal investigations."

Karen nodded approvingly. "That's good. And can the pathologist get in there as well?"

"Yep, Izzy can go ahead as well."

It was good news for Karen. The investigation could start. With the crime scene under full scrutiny, she also needed to get her team to trace the car that ran Marcus and Natasha off the road. It was a crucial element in their enquiry. She needed to know whether it was connected to the arson attack. It could have been a local who knew the road well and was driving like an idiot, but a thought niggled the back of her mind that perhaps it was the suspect fleeing the scene.

Thanking Janet for all her help and insights as the investigator loaded up her van, Karen was just about to grab some refreshments when she stopped in mid-step. Several of the other officers around her also paused in reflection as three black vans pulled into the courtyard and reversed their vehicles towards the farmhouse before coming to a gentle stop. The words "Private Ambulance" were printed on the sides of each van. Two men exited each vehicle, dressed in matching black two-piece suits, white shirts and black ties. Each pair walked around to the rear of the vehicles before opening the double doors and pulling out a stretcher with a black body bag on it in readiness for when they could remove the bodies.

It wouldn't be long before Karen got the answers she needed. Izzy had already promised her she would start the first of the post-mortems tomorrow and she expected it would take a few days to do all six victims.

Karen had a cup of tea in one hand, and a ham sandwich in the other. She murmured to herself, savouring every mouthful. It wasn't until she had eaten that she realised how ravenous she was. A ham sandwich had never tasted so good, she mused, especially when washed down with a sip of sweet tea. She enjoyed every mouthful and could feel her energy levels rising. The weariness that she had felt over the last few hours melted away.

The courtyard fell silent sometime later when the first stretcher came out with the twisted remains of a victim. The body bag took on a macabre shape as if the corpse was trying to punch its way out. The moment wasn't lost on Karen as she looked around to see a few officers bowing their heads in respect. It was a painful moment for all of them.

8

KAREN TRUDGED through the desks of the SCU, the Special Crime Unit, towards the front where she'd set up additional whiteboards and maps after her long day at the farmhouse. An early start yesterday, little to eat, and on her feet all day, had left her achy and weary. She felt like the stuffing from a cushion had been jammed between her ears. Two cups of black strong coffee had done little to shake off the fog.

The team gathered around and perched on the edge of the desks closest to her, whilst others wheeled chairs into the spaces between the desks. With the sun rising early this morning, the heat of summer was in full swing, and though it was already hot outside, the office was cool thanks to the air conditioning. Karen recalled several stations she had worked in where air conditioning didn't exist. Officers had relied on open windows and desk fans to battle through the London heat, which was often stifling and intense.

The usual suspects gathered closest to her. Jade was to her left. Ed, Belinda, and Ty formed a small arc in front of her.

Her latest recruits, Preet and Ned, were scattered amongst the other dozen officers who were in for the day shift.

Karen picked up a brown envelope and removed photographs from it. One by one, she attached them to the whiteboard. Each one made her pause as she blinked hard through the shock that reminded her of yesterday. Faint murmurings rippled behind her from her assembled team.

"Right, everyone, this is challenging for us." As Karen scanned the sea of faces, she noticed that most weren't even looking at her. Many stared in disbelief at the images, their mouths hanging, a few shaking their heads. Karen stepped to one side of the whiteboard, took a sip of her coffee and cleared her throat. "As you can see, it wasn't a pretty sight yesterday. These are the images taken by SOCO who worked through the night. We'll need to begin identifying these victims, but as you can tell, we have little to go on." Karen took a moment to check that everyone was okay before she continued. Ned, her new trainee detective constable, often shortened to TDC, looked shocked and shaken by the images. His eyes were wide as he chewed on his bottom lip.

Karen handed out a stack of information which was passed amongst the officers. "Janet, the fire investigator, confirmed that this wasn't an accident but a case of arson. Someone intended to harm the Lawson family. It's all detailed in the handout. We are dealing with three genera-tions of a family wiped out. You can see from Janet's report why she concluded it was indeed arson, so I won't go over it again, but take the time to read through that."

"Someone with a grudge?" an officer piped up from the back.

Karen shrugged a shoulder. "It's one motive. As yet, it's early days, so it's hard to determine the motive, but yes, a grudge is a theory."

"Why did they die in their beds? Wouldn't they have tried to escape?" another asked.

"Depends if they died before the fire was started." Ty replied.

Karen agreed. "That's what we need to find out. We've only got evidence to suggest that one occupant tried to escape." Karen pointed to the photographs in the pack and indicated the hand marks and scratches on the window, and the further signs found on the wall beneath it. She then simulated what might have happened, showing that the hands were dragged down the wall. "We believe that was William Lawson, the grandfather. He was elderly and needed a wheelchair to help him get around. They found a body beside that wheelchair, its hand wrapped around the frame."

"So, he wasn't able to rouse the others?" Belinda thought aloud.

Karen perched on a table nearby and shook her head. "If I'm honest, we don't know. That's what our investigation needs to uncover. Were they drugged? Which is why they didn't respond to the fire? Were they already dead? And the fire was an attempt to cover over whatever had happened before? We have so many questions that we need answers to."

"So, where do we start?" Ed asked.

"I need the team to look for next of kin. We also need to look for any evidence of run-ins with other farmers, locals, outsiders, even suppliers. Did they kick travellers off their land? Have other farmers experienced issues with travellers? I remember a case in Essex a few years back where a landowner served a court order to have a group of travellers removed from his land. The poor bloke was beaten to a pulp just days later. Look at every angle. We need a full rundown on the family. Got that?" Karen asked no one in particular.

Many officers nodded their heads as they continued to take notes.

"Check their finances as well. Had they run up any debts? Look at the financials of the farm. Was it running in profit? Were profits sliding? Had anyone else invested in the farm and perhaps fallen out with the Lawsons? Can you see where I'm going with this? I want a full background check and picture built up of the Lawson farm."

"I'll organise a few of us to look at the individual members of the family," Jade said. "Maybe there was something going on with the sons or daughter."

"Jealous lover?" Ed chipped in. "Maybe the husband or wife were having an affair which turned sour, and the lover sought revenge?"

Karen loved how her team was examining this from all angles. "These are credible ideas worth checking out. Let's get started and see what we can uncover. I'm heading back to the farmhouse, and though I'm not looking forward to it, I'll be at the first post-mortem later today. I'm hoping once we've got the first one out of the way, we may have some new leads. Of course, any of you are more than welcome to take my place at the PM?" Karen suggested, scanning her officers. Some looked down at their notes, others turned to look out of the nearest window, and the rest stared at her with blank faces. Karen laughed. "I thought there wouldn't be a queue of volunteers." Karen scanned her team. "Tyler, sorry mate, you'll be at the PM with me. Okay, let's get to work. We'll have another briefing tomorrow morning to review what we've got so far."

As her officers filtered back to their desks, Karen turned to look at the whiteboard again. Her eyes moved from one picture to another. One blackened and twisted body after another. Their identities unrecognisable, their genders erased, their skin melted and cracked like the charring on a slab of burnt brisket. Karen felt sickened to the pit of her stomach.

9

AFTER WRAPPING up the team briefing, Karen made her way along the corridors towards Detective Superintendent Laura Kelly's office. Having been here for a few months now, Karen was becoming familiar with the officers, especially some of the senior ones, and as she passed them, they exchanged pleasantries with her. If anything, it made her feel more welcome. She had formed the opinion that not only was it a slower pace of life up here compared to London, but officers had more time to stop and talk to you regardless of rank.

From her days in London, Karen had learned a very much head down, get on with work approach. With the Met being the largest police force in the UK, and with her work taking her from station to station, it had been not only hard to form friendships, but just as hard to cement working relationships. She could stop and talk to an officer and then not see their face again for months, if ever. It was impersonal and made the job even harder. With senior officers being so busy and under both internal and public pressure, there was often the sense of every person for themselves. There had been several occasions where she'd been stabbed in the back by colleagues who were more interested in self-preservation than anything else.

The ugly spectre of DCI Skelton loomed into her awareness. Her thoughts soured as she thought of the man. Skelton had almost sunk her career, which was bad enough. But he'd had blood on his hands as he had sacrificed fellow officers to protect his own arse. Karen had skirted death on a number of occasions due to him, and she wasn't unhappy that his reign of greed, terror, and violence had ended in a hail of bullets.

Karen found the door to Kelly's office open, with her boss striding around her office, reading a memo in her hands. As Karen knocked on the door, Kelly spun round and looked up.

"Sorry, Karen. I didn't realise you were there. I've got another management meeting after lunch and there's a ton of stuff I need to read through ahead of it."

"Oh, I don't want to interrupt you. I can always pop back later."

Kelly walked around to the other side of the desk and dropped into her chair. She waved away Karen's concern and asked her to take a seat. Her eyes narrowed as she studied Karen. "Is everything okay?" she asked, leaning forward and resting her elbows on the desk before interlocking her fingers.

"Um, yes. I'm okay." Karen stiffened, wondering where this was going. She could never anticipate Kelly's thoughts because her concerned smiles often masked the true intention behind her questions.

"No reason. You look... well... exhausted. You're not working too hard, are you?"

Karen was about to reply when Kelly continued.

"You have been through a lot, and I understand if you have days where everything feels overwhelming. You know you can talk to me, don't you?"

"Of course, ma'am," Karen responded cautiously.

Kelly sat up quickly, all bright and breezy. "Good. I heard all about the fire yesterday. Were you there all day?"

"Yes, ma'am. I think that's why I look like a sack of shit today, pardon my French."

Kelly raised a hand and waved off Karen's apology.

Karen updated Kelly with the bones of the case, and how the fire was now a case of arson and multiple homicides.

"Yes. I reviewed the body cam footage this morning. Quite a horrific scene."

"It was. Especially because it's in such an idyllic rural setting. Bart's team were there all night, and they'll remain there for another day or two. It's a large crime scene. We're not just looking at the farmhouse but the connected outbuildings and surrounding land. I've organised extra resources to help us with the search."

Kelly heartily nodded and added that she was glad to assign extra resources if necessary.

"I've got the first of the PMs this afternoon, and it will not be a pretty one either. Tyler is joining me."

Kelly offered a reassuring smile. "The team coping with this okay?"

"Yes, ma'am. They're a seasoned bunch but saddened at the loss of six lives in such a horrific way. Mind you, I think my new TDC found it hard looking at the images provided by Bart's team. They were pretty grim. I'm going to make sure he's okay before I head out."

"Do you know much about the family yet?" Kelly asked, shuffling her papers together and sliding them into a brown Manila folder.

"No, other than it was the Lawson family. We're about to build up a full victimology on each member. We need to find out if the whole family was the intended target or one individual, with the other five members being collateral damage."

Kelly was pensive for a moment as she hung on Karen's words, digesting them. "Arson attacks are always difficult to examine and solve. Vendettas, greed, jealousy, debts, fraud and revenge need to be examined. It could also have been a prank by local kids that went terribly wrong. It's not unheard of." Kelly sighed as she stared up at the ceiling. "In past cases, they have set hay barns alight, joy-ridden farm machinery and then set them alight, sheep and cattle have been attacked and butchered in the fields... And for what? A laugh." Kelly spat out the last two words as her features stiffened.

"I hadn't thought of the prank angle as much, but that's an excellent suggestion, and I'll take that on board, ma'am. We haven't got access to much CCTV, so that's hampering the initial evidence gathering. But I took a moment to stop and check out a farm shop that belonged to them. They had window displays showing off their awards for innovation, management of dairy cattle, and cheese production."

Kelly stood, signalling the end as she gathered her papers together. "Keep me updated. I need to grab a coffee and review my management information one last time before my meeting."

10

KAREN MADE her way through the narrow winding country lanes, but still wasn't comfortable driving on them. With such tall hedgerows and sharp bends, it was often hard to see approaching vehicles until it was too late. As she experienced fast-approaching oncoming vehicles that did little to slow down or pull over, she imagined Marcus and Natasha in the same situation. It had crossed her mind a few times to flick on her blue lights to annoy them.

"Anyone would think we're at a track day at Silverstone with the way these idiots drive," Karen hissed, as she hugged the inside of a tight left bend when she saw an approaching hay truck coming towards her.

Jade, who she'd picked up on her way to the crime scene, laughed from the passenger seat as she looked ahead to see the driver mouthing an obscenity at them whilst sticking up a finger in their direction. "Oh, the joys of country living. Still, it beats the noisy, busy, choking pollution of London, don't you think?"

Jade had a point. At some stage, Karen would have to get used to the fact that driving on country lanes meant taking her life in her own hands, as locals seemed to drive without giving a crap about anyone else.

Karen pulled through the farm gate and into the courtyard that she had only left a few hours ago. There was a different feel to the place today. There wasn't the sense of urgency and horror that had greeted her yesterday. Everything seemed quieter and more thoughtful. She also noticed that there was a visible lack of curious onlookers that so often loitered around crime scenes. There were no locals gathering in small huddles and talking in hushed tones. But she had noticed a few flowers that had been left on the roadside by the entrance to the farm.

As Karen and Jade stepped from the car, the smell of burnt timber lingered in the air. To the far end of the courtyard, two police vans had taken up position, and a dozen officers in overalls were being briefed on the search grids they needed to cover starting with the farm buildings, before moving to the adjoining garden and fields.

Though it was good to see the extra resources, she knew she would need more to cover the area, and made a mental note to call Kelly.

"Back again, Karen?" Bart shouted as he made his way over to Karen and Jade.

"You know me. You can't keep me away from a good crime scene," Karen replied. "How are you getting on?"

Bart stopped beside them, and the three of them stood in a single line facing the farmhouse.

"We're changing over shifts. The team was sent home in the early hours and replaced by fresh officers. But a few are needed elsewhere, so I've drafted in further manpower."

"Can we get in there to have a look around?" Karen asked.

Bart nodded. "Sure, just be careful where you tread. It's still wet in places. I've got various team members scattered throughout the building, but they'll tell you if you get in their way."

Bart provided Karen and Jade with hard hats from his van before they followed him into the building.

"You've had all the information from Janet, haven't you?" Bart asked, glancing over his shoulder in Karen's direction.

Karen nodded.

Bart led them through the building. "We have made the place safe," he said, stepping over a few charred pieces of timber, his feet splashing into a puddle of blackened water. "They assessed the structural damage, dealt with the damaged electricity and gas mains, moved the hazardous debris, and removed any dangerous combustible products or toxic substances."

"Glad to hear it. The last thing I want to do is go up like a Roman candle," Karen said, her dark humour causing Jade to roll her eyes.

Having guided them upstairs, Bart allowed Karen and Jade to take the lead. "Until now, we've closely controlled the crime scene to preserve evidence and get it documented properly. We've also produced a plan of the farmhouse, including the location of objects and bodies, and backed it up with photographic evidence as well. Obviously, you must take into consideration that there's been considerable disturbance caused by the fire service as they brought the fire under control." Bart paused for a moment to examine fire damage to the walls before he continued. "We've completed the external examination of the scene, including all the doors and windows. We didn't find any tools that may have been used to gain access to the building. But as we already know, the side door was open and most likely the point of entry."

Karen listened with one ear as Bart gave them a running commentary, but her mind was processing the scene again in the fire's aftermath. She glanced across to see Jade also lost deep in thought, her eyes scanning the floor, the walls, and then the ceiling of each room that they passed. Karen entered the nearest bedroom, her mind conjuring up a flashback of the twisted, burnt remains of two victims lying side by side in bed. By now, Jade had left the room and entered the adjoining one. Karen caught up with her and stopped in the doorway. This was the bedroom where they'd discovered the presumed body of William Lawson just inches from the burnt-out metal frame of a wheelchair. Karen remembered seeing the deformed, blackened fingers grasping the frame. The final desperate moments of a victim trying to escape the oncoming inferno.

The rubber from the wheels of the wheelchair had melted and formed hard, lumpy bumps on the floor.

"I'm so sorry you had to see this," Jade said, turning towards Karen. "It's terrible seeing it now but having seen it with the bodies still in situ, that's awful," Jade added, pursing her lips into a thin line.

Karen took in a sharp intake of breath. "It wasn't good." She demonstrated how the body had been positioned, and its proximity to the window whilst indicating the finger trail marks that ran down the wall.

"Did someone murder them in their beds, and perhaps this victim was attacked, but had survived, only to die in the fire?" Jade speculated. "The windows were unlocked in the bedrooms, so it could explain why the other members of the family didn't escape."

"Yeah, maybe," Karen replied, lost in her own thoughts. They made their way through the remaining first-floor rooms before coming back down and wandering around the lounge and kitchen for a second time. The wine bottles that Karen remembered from her first visit had been removed for forensic analysis, the clean outline of where the bottles once rested remaining on the table. Two SOCOs were examining the window ledges in the lounge using high-powered torches. It was reassuring to know that every square inch of the property was being subjected to a detailed scrutiny to pick up every shred of evidence before it was destroyed any further.

"Did you find a dog?" Jade shouted from the kitchen.

Karen left the lounge and walked through to the kitchen; curiosity etched on her features as she grimaced. "Come to think of it, no. Why?"

Jade pointed to the floor. "Dog bowl."

Karen's eyes widened. "Every farmer generally has a dog or two. Where's this one?" she muttered, walking towards the kitchen window and staring out across the garden. Karen pulled out her phone and searched for Ellen's number before calling it.

"Ellen speaking."

"Hi, Ellen. This is DCI Karen Heath. We met yesterday at the Lawson farm."

"Yes, how can I help?"

"The Lawsons. We found a dog bowl, so I assume they have a dog? But we haven't found one on the premises."

"Ah, shit. They have a dog, a collie named Bonnie."

"One sec, Ellen," Karen said as she headed towards the back door of the kitchen and stepped out into the garden. "Bonnie!" Karen shouted. She called out again several times before returning to her conversation. "She's not responding. Maybe she's hiding, or run away?"

"You're probably right. I imagine she was terrified. I'm hoping she's somewhere on the farm. I doubt she would have gone far, especially if she was injured. I'm just dealing with a few things at the moment at another farm that I help out on, but I can pop back a little later and have a look? She knows me very well. If she's around, she might come to me."

"That would be really helpful, Ellen. Can you let me know if you find her?"

"Of course."

"The poor dog must be terrified," Jade remarked. "Do you want me to hang around and look for her?"

Karen shook her head. "No, don't worry about it. Come on. I need to get back as I'm meeting Zac for lunch."

11

KAREN CHECKED the time on her phone as she raced from her car and headed for the station canteen to meet her boyfriend, DCI Zac Walker, the man behind her move to York after they'd worked on a case together She was late, a habit that was becoming all too frequent in her life. Whether it was getting up and out of her apartment on time each morning, or coming over to Zac's in the evening, or just a simple lunch, life had a habit of getting in the way. Karen darted through the double doors of the canteen, colliding with two officers coming the other way.

"Sorry... Sorry," Karen exclaimed, as one officer rubbed his arm from where the door slammed into him.

Luckily for Karen, he saw the funny side of it and made an off-the-cuff remark Karen didn't pick up. Spotting Zac off to her left, Karen darted between the different dining tables as she approached Zac. Frustration was etched on his face as he rolled his eyes.

"Sorry... I'm so sorry. For Christ's sake, that's all I seem to say at the moment," Karen said, pulling out a chair opposite Zac. She would have loved to have leant over and kissed him because he looked so gorgeous, but she doubted if it would go down very well with the rest of her colleagues in the canteen.

"Your timekeeping is dismal. I've called you four times and there was no answer." Zac tutted.

"I know. I was back at the farmhouse and got stuck behind a large tractor thing with a ton of spikes on wheels."

Zac's shoulders bounced as he laughed silently. "Is that the technical term?"

Karen sat back in her chair. "Listen, I'm no farmer. I'm sure that monstrosity has its uses. For what, I'm not sure, but it blocked the track. It was touching the hedgerows on both sides. Thankfully, I was behind it, but I felt sorry for the oncoming cars."

Zac pushed across a ham and pickle sandwich in its plastic wrapper, and a carton of apple juice. "It's not the Ritz, but this will have to do."

Karen tore open the wrapper and pulled out the sandwich. Her eyes widened as she took an enormous bite. She closed her eyes as she savoured the sandwich before letting out a gentle moan. "Oh, trust me. When you're bloody starving, nothing beats a ham and pickle sandwich."

Zac had already finished his lunch and sipped on his coffee whilst they caught up. "How's the investigation going? Have you made any progress?"

Karen shrugged as she wiped a few crumbs from her lips with the back of her hand. "Not much. Arson. Six indistinguishable bodies. Three generations wiped out. No CCTV capturing intruders to the farmhouse. No witnesses. No motive. Next question?"

"Oh. That good?"

Karen pulled a face. "Yep. I have diddly-squat apart from a ton of cow crap all over my shoes. This one is going to be down to good old-fashioned policing. Asking lots of questions and doing some serious digging into the backgrounds of the victims. As it stands, we don't know if the whole family was the target of the arson attack, or whether one of the six was the intended victim. We really don't know."

"Worth putting out an appeal for information?" Zac suggested. "I think you'll find that farmers are very good at knowing what their neighbours are up to. Both professionally and personally. Most of it is with good intent, but the greedy ones like to keep tabs on their neighbours... If you know what I mean."

"Definitely. I need to get the case logged with Crimestoppers. Then I'll leave it a few days because I want to see what the post-mortems and forensics throw up. I think I will go to the press after that, but I'll need to get Laura on my side first."

Zac agreed it was an excellent strategy to start with. He also suggested that if she needed help to build bridges with a few of the local farmers, then he was happy to help.

Karen changed the subject as she grabbed the second half of her sandwich and devoured it, whilst also checking the time on her phone. "It was good fun going down to see Tommy and his family wasn't it?"

Zac nodded and smiled.

A few weeks ago, they'd taken up DI Tommy Nugent's offer to come down and spend a weekend with him and his family. Karen had loved seeing Tommy again. It was as if time had stood still as they laughed and reminisced about their early days in the Met. She was just as delighted that Zac had enjoyed his time down there getting to know Tommy, his wife Erin, and their daughter Fran.

"Yes. It was nice being by the coast. Can't beat a bit of fresh sea air. Loved Durdle Door and Lulworth Cove. It was nice of Tommy to show us around. Nice fella," Zac said. "Though I wasn't too sure about his mother-in-law. She certainly knows how to wind Tommy up."

Karen laughed. Carol Driscoll, Erin's mother, lived with them. The older woman was widowed, arthritic, and played on the fact that she was getting forgetful so couldn't remember Tommy's name. "Well, he's invited us down again when we get a chance. Perhaps we could do a half-term break and get an Airbnb? What are you doing about the summer holidays? School will break up soon."

Zac pursed his lips and stared out of the window beside them. "I'm not sure yet. I need to ask. I don't know if her mum has anything planned for her but going by how frosty things have been between her and Michelle, I'm not sure Summer wants to spend any time with her. How about if we take Summer away for a week or two? Are you ready for a family holiday yet?" Zac winked.

The suggestion took Karen by surprise. As the months passed by, Karen slipped into more "family" situations. Though it had terrified her at first, she'd become used to it, often reflecting on how she'd softened so much in so little time. It was as if she had changed into an absolutely different Karen, and left the foul-mouthed, aggressive, heavy drinking, and promiscuous Karen far behind.

"It's a lovely idea, and I would love to, but I think you need to spend some quality time with Summer. Just the two of you. She has had a rough time of it with her mum, and maybe what she needs now is quality daddy and daughter time?" Karen suggested.

"Maybe. But I'd love you there, and I know Summer would too."

"That's nice of you to say. Maybe next time," Karen replied with a sigh as she realised the time. "I've got to head back out again. Will call you later," she said, rising from her chair.

"You better," Zac replied, following her out.

12

HAVING LEFT ZAC AFTER LUNCH, Karen made her way to the Wagstaff farm. The journey didn't take longer than fifteen minutes as she relied on her satnav to guide her through the narrow country lanes. She knew it wasn't far from the Lawson farm since Ellen had guided the Lawsons' herd across a few fields towards the Wagstaffs adjoining land.

Her mind travelled back to the conversation with Zac and his offer of a family holiday with himself and Summer. Every part of her had wanted to agree when Zac had suggested the idea, her heart flipping in her chest at the prospect, but she'd had to pull away from it. After every-thing that Summer had been through, Karen knew Summer needed time to bond with her dad and her going too would be nothing more than a distraction. There would be other times, Karen told herself.

Directions to Wagstaff farm proved simple enough when she spotted a sign in the hedgerow showing that the entrance was one hundred yards further up on the left.

Karen slowed, her eyes scanning the hedgerow looking for the gap. Having spotted it at the last moment, Karen did a sharp left and swung into a gravel driveway. The farm looked bigger than the Lawsons'. There were two houses sitting side by side and various barns in an L-shaped layout to her right. Karen stopped her car alongside a black pickup truck, which had a small flatbed trailer hooked up to it. She glanced across and judging from the scattering of straw, it was used to transport hay bales around the farm.

Stepping from her vehicle, she made her way towards a small building to the left of one property which had a sign above it reading, "Farm Office". She was pleased by the absence of puddles of cowpat and concluded that the "dirty" side of the business took place around the back of the farmhouses where she could hear the noise of cows.

Upon entering through the office door, Karen noticed three desks, two piled high with paperwork, the third with a thin, ruddy-faced man wearing a flat cap. He sat behind it staring at a computer screen. Karen pulled out her warrant card.

"Hi, there. I'm Detective Chief Inspector Karen Heath from York police. I'm investigating the fire at the Lawsons'. You are?"

The man stood and extended his hand. "Charles Wagstaff. Owner. I run this farm with my wife, Jenny."

Confirming that she had found the right person, Karen shook his hand and noticed the roughness. His skin was dry, tough and leathery, with calluses on his palms, no doubt the result from spending all of his working life outdoors. "I wonder if you could help us with our enquiries? We're trying to build a picture of the Lawson family."

Charles rubbed his stubbly chin. His upper lids drooped heavily over his eyes, but he gazed at Karen from beneath them. "Awful news. I'm really shocked. We all are. It's not what you hear about that often."

"I understand Ellen brought their herd here to be milked?"

Charles nodded and grimaced. "It's the least I could do. We've got a better set-up here."

"How so?" Karen asked.

"We milk a hundred and eighty pedigree Holstein Friesians. Before we had an abreast parlour with six units which were at least forty years old. It was very manual and took over four hours to milk the herd twice a day. We replaced it about two years ago with a rapid exit parlour which speeded everything up by fifty per cent." Charles zipped up his jacket and headed for the front door asking Karen to join him. "It's also a healthier working environment," he said, stepping into the open. "The cows come in and turn so their back legs are just there and you can put the unit on. It makes it so much easier, and we save a fortune in labour costs."

"So, you had the spare capacity to help?"

"Pretty much. We like to help each other around here. We sometimes share machinery, help each other out when we've got a problem on our farms. *Most* of us round here are more than willing to lend a hand."

Karen spotted the change in his tone. She followed Charles as he headed around the back of the buildings, where the noise of the herd grew louder. She paused for a moment as Charles walked across the concrete yard, his feet squelching in the cow shit that littered the floor.

Charles stopped and glanced over his shoulder. The older man laughed when he saw Karen staring at the floor around her as if she had stepped into the middle of a minefield, scared where to place her feet. "Come on. It won't hurt you. Breathe it in!" Charles inhaled deeply and closed his eyes blissfully. "Fresh country air."

Karen pulled a face as the smell of rotten eggs crawled up her body and clawed at her nose. "Can't we go back to your office and continue the conversation?"

Charles rested his hands on his hips and looked on in bewilderment. "As a young child I lived out in the countryside on my parents' cattle farm. The neighbouring farm turned some of their milk into ice cream which they sold on site. As a treat, my parents would take us for ice cream at the farm. Thus, my first exposure to both the taste of ice cream and the smell of cow shit happened at the same time." Charles's shoulders bounced as he chuckled to himself at the memory. "And so, like some kind of scatty Pavlovian, now whenever I walk through a field and smell shit, I think of ice cream and feel warm and happy."

Karen grimaced, still minding her step as she caught up.

"You should be grateful you're not in India. Cows and *their* by-products are sacred and holy. They distil cow's urine and drink the stuff. In Indian prayers, they use cow urine and cowpats. It's even sold on Amazon, check it out. This stuff is valuable," Charles said, staring at the floor.

Karen diverted her attention from the thoughts that were forming in her mind. "How well did you know the Lawsons?"

"Pretty good. We both use Ellen as an extra pair of hands. And because our farms back out on to each other, I saw John and his family often."

"Were they well liked around here?" Karen asked.

Charles shrugged. "As far as I know. I didn't hear a bad word being said against them. Old man Lawson was well respected round here until he retired and handed the business over to John."

"Did you hear or see anything on the night of the fire? Or perhaps in the days preceding the fire? Maybe anyone lurking around the fields that shouldn't have been there?"

Charles narrowed his eyes as he thought about it before shaking his head.

"Did they have any arguments or run-ins with anyone?"

"Not as far as I know, DCI Heath. Not enough to warrant their place being torched. They didn't get on well with Dixon, another local farmer, but then again, most of us don't, including me."

"Why not?"

"It's simple. He's not a true farmer. He is purely driven by profit. I have little to do with him personally. I'm just saying what I heard."

Charles's answers bothered Karen. Not because she doubted his honesty, but because everything she was hearing suggested that the Lawsons were good people, which meant the maliciousness of the attack troubled her further.

"Okay, Mr Wagstaff. That's really helpful. Is Ellen around? I wouldn't mind having a word with her whilst I'm here."

"I'm afraid not," he said, shaking his head. "Should be back later to help with the evening milking, if you'd like to pop back?"

"Thank you. I'll try calling her first, but the reception seems to be very patchy around here. So I might pop back," Karen said, shaking Charles's hand before returning to her car.

13

KAREN WAITED outside the hospital mortuary, checking her phone every few minutes. Tyler had texted her to say that he was looking for a parking space and shouldn't be much longer. When he joined her, they headed to an adjoining room within the mortuary, where they were given face masks and green gowns to wear.

The sound of music grew louder as Karen walked down the corridor with Tyler. They entered the first examination room to find Izzy Armitage, the pathologist, whistling to the background music as she leant over the blackened remains of the first cadaver.

"Sorry we're late, Izzy. Too much to do or not enough time."

Izzy looked up from her examination and nodded as her face mask puffed in and out with each breath. "No worries. We've only started. Just to give you a quick heads-up, we haven't done all the normal visual identification and measurements, for obvious reasons."

Karen came around to the other side of the table, with Tyler standing beside her but further back. She took a moment to examine the twisted and charred remains of the body. During the fire, the body had contorted into what was known as the "pugilist" or "boxer" pose—where differential heat-related contraction of the muscles caused a characteristic position of the limbs. Karen noticed the arms were flexed at the elbows and raised towards the ceiling, with the legs pulled in closer to the abdomen. The sight was always difficult for Karen to cope with. She had attended dozens of post-mortems in her time, but the victims of arson were always the most challenging ones.

"As you can tell, it's difficult to prove whether this is a male or female body, but I believe it's male because they have a smaller pelvis, and it's designed differently. If there had been only limited fire damage to the body, then it may have been possible for us to get the visual identification of the deceased. We have shrinkage of the internal organs. Their height and weight can't be determined because of the heat-related shrinkage and shortening of the body and fluid weight loss through evaporation. I'm unable to determine hair or eye colour, any tattoos or scars, or fingerprints. But we may be able to extract bone marrow tissue from deeper within the body cavity for DNA identification."

Karen nodded as her eyes travelled up and down the body. There was no evidence of genitalia or breasts. The body reminded her of a mummified corpse that had been burnt. "Well, that's made our job even harder. Dental records?"

Izzy nodded as she leant in closer to the cadaver's head, her face a few inches away. "Providing the tooth enamel is intact and has survived the extreme heat. I can preserve the teeth before an odontological examination by spraying them with a lacquer spray. Tooth enamel can become very fragile when exposed to extreme heat and shatter, so I'll do my best."

"Thanks, Izzy. That would be helpful." Karen glanced over her shoulder towards Tyler, who remained tight-lipped. His eyes remained transfixed on the body; his face taut and pale. "You okay, Tyler?" Karen asked.

Tyler didn't take his eyes off the body but nodded once.

They both observed over the next thirty minutes as Izzy continued with her examination. At one point, Izzy had to use considerable force to make an incision through the breastplate to access the lungs. She murmured the odd word to herself as her examination shifted from the chest to the throat and then to the face, before dropping from the torso and back down to the victim's feet.

Izzy stepped back and blew out her cheeks. "I can't find any other patterns of injury. There're no lacerations, incisions, or old scars that I can see. There is what we call arte-factual injury," she said, stepping back towards the table and pointing to several areas around the body where there had been heat-induced splitting of the skin resembling lacerations.

"So as far as we can tell, nothing suggests that this victim was attacked and murdered prior to the fire?" Karen asked for clarification.

"Not as far as I can see. I'll look elsewhere by trying to take a blood sample from any preserved tissue to estimate the carboxyhaemoglobin levels. Anything exceeding fifty per cent will be evidence that the deceased was alive when the fire initiated, which I'm positive of since there is evidence of soot in the airways, especially below the level of the vocal cords, and combined with the mucus in the distal airways."

Karen folded her arms across her chest. This was precisely what she needed. "So they died of smoke inhalation?"

"Yes. I'll request the usual tox analysis too if I can get a decent sample. Worth checking for anything else in the blood. Though I still need to do a post-mortem on the other five victims, I imagine the outcome will be the same. I guess that's a blessing of sorts. They were dead before the fire got to them."

Karen thanked Izzy before leaving her to finish her examination.

Ty stood by the entrance to the hospital and stared off into the distance. Cars circled up and down aisles looking for that elusive parking space that never materialised. Patients stood to one side puffing on a cheeky fag, and relatives wandered in ahead of visiting hours. Life went on.

"Wasn't easy, hey?" Karen said as she paused alongside him.

Ty shook his head. "Does it ever get easier? That was horrific."

"First burns vic?"

"Yeah." Ty took in a deep breath and blew out. "I feel sick to the pit of my stomach. It was just so... sad."

"It means you're still human, and that's a good thing. We harden up through our careers because of all the shit we see, but it doesn't stop us from feeling all the human emotions. I won't lie. I've cried after a few PMs. Especially kids. One of these days you'll need a good cry too. Don't be scared or embarrassed about that. Okay?"

"I'll try. Thanks, Karen."

Karen stepped in closer and elbowed Ty in his side. "Come on. I'll buy you a coffee."

14

THE MOMENT KAREN returned to the Wagstaff farm, the residual warmth from the day hung in the air and surrounded her as she stepped out of her car. Karen was certain the heat of the summer was building. The morning sun was stronger, the air drier, and she couldn't step out into the open without a pair of sunglasses to shield her eyes. A part of her wanted to stay in the car and enjoy the cooling breeze of the air conditioning on her face. The argument that raged in her mind only intensified when she noticed thick swarms of flies buzzing around her. She batted them away with her hand as she headed to the farm office.

Being only too pleased to see her again, Charles Wagstaff pointed her in the direction of the milking parlour where she would find Ellen.

Karen hovered by the entrance to the parlour, the smell an invisible barrier holding her back from venturing in any further. She spotted Ellen towards the far end, a large broom in one hand, a hosepipe on the floor beside her feet.

Thankfully for Karen, there was a distinct absence of cows, but they'd certainly left their mark on the floor. She shouted to Ellen, hoping that Ellen would join her by the entrance, but her hope was short-lived when Ellen waved her over saying that she didn't have time to stop.

Karen groaned as she stepped through watery puddles, not wishing to imagine what they were, but judging by the smell, she had a pretty good idea. Thankfully, she had just bought a pair of wellies and had slipped them on when leaving the car. She had lost count of the number of times she had been caught short when attending crime scenes that were more remote, dirty, wet, or muddy. Whilst in London, she hadn't contemplated investing in them, but having found herself in several sticky situations where her shoes had been ruined, and no doubt the laughing stock of local officers, she'd resigned herself to buying a pair of green wellies which were unflattering whichever angle she looked at them in the mirror.

"Hi, Ellen. Sorry to disturb you. I wanted to catch up with you."

"I know. Charles said you'd stopped by. I picked up a few missed calls from you earlier on this evening. I've been out moving a flock of ninety sheep and getting them marked up at another farm, and the signal is rubbish."

"It sounds like you're always on the go," Karen said as she glanced around the milking parlour. She didn't have a clue what all the equipment was, or how to use it, but she carried huge respect for Ellen as she watched her go about her work.

"It's part of our evening routine. Charles likes the milking done around four or five p.m. After that, we typically just clean the cubicles down and push the slurry out. The herd are returned to the fields to graze and sleep and then we start it all over again with milking at six a.m. But we're having to double up as we've got the Lawsons' herd here. The cows have a great body clock, so when milking time comes around, they queue ready to come in. There are certain cows who are always at the front. At Charles's farm, we always expect to see Dottie and Lacey leading the herd in to be milked."

Karen smiled at the thought that each cow had a name. As she followed Ellen up and down the walkways whilst the woman hosed and swept, she wondered if they were all given names, and then how on earth did Charles and Ellen either remember or recognise each cow.

"How's the investigation going?" Ellen asked.

"It's still early days, and we're gathering as much information as possible, which is why I wanted to talk to you," Karen said, changing direction. "What can you tell me about the Lawsons?"

Ellen paused for a moment and rested her hands on the top of the broom handle. "A nice family. Hard-working. They kept themselves to themselves. Time permitting, they turned up at the farming conventions and festivals. Pretty successful. Keen to innovate and diversify whilst also upholding the true values of farming. I think you have to these days."

"Sounds like they had it all sorted?"

Ellen thought for a moment before nodding. "Yes. They have a solid milking operation. The herd are healthy and strong. A good relationship with their suppliers too."

Karen followed Ellen out into the open and enjoyed the fresh air. "Any enemies or fallouts?"

"Enemies... Not as far as I'm aware. Mind you, if they did, I don't think John... John Lawson," Ellen added for clarification, "would have said anything. He was a proud man and always kept things professional... and ethical."

"And fallouts?"

"I wouldn't say fallouts. You do occasionally disagree with a fellow farmer over things like the purchasing price of cattle or who gets first dibs on a tractor that they might be sharing. Dixon has a large farm next to John. I know Dixon had asked a few times if John was interested in selling, but John turned him down. It was a family farm. Been with them for a few generations, and John was keen to pass it down to the next generation of his family."

Karen made a mental note to follow up on the Dixon line of enquiry. "Any other next of kin?"

"John has an older brother, Daniel. He lives in Wales, married a sheep farmer. They've got a thriving alpaca trekking business as well, of all things."

"Alpaca trekking? That's a new one on me," Karen said.

Ellen shrugged. "All the rage, from what I can gather. Alpaca trekking. Alpaca wool. I know little about it myself. But I would say that John's business was going places. They had plans for growth and expansion above and beyond just the dairy business. That's what I liked about John and his family. They had vision." Ellen smiled. "They wanted to keep traditional dairy farming alive whilst also finding other business opportunities that sat comfortably with what they stood for. There was talk of setting up a glamping business on their land, where guests could help with duties on the farm to give them a more unique experience of rural life."

Listening to Ellen gave Karen an opportunity to build a more detailed understanding of the farming family. The more she heard, the more she wondered why anyone would want to harm them unless... someone was jealous of their success and drive. She'd heard nothing yet from her various conversations to suspect the Lawsons of any wrongdoing.

"It sounds like they were a good family," Karen remarked.

Ellen let out a long sigh. "They were. And the sad thing is that forty-eight hours ago they had just won a contract to supply their own cheese to a local chain of supermarkets. It was a big win for them."

That would explain the wine bottles. A celebration, Karen thought as she thanked Ellen for her time before making her way back to the car and heading home for the evening.

15

KAREN WOKE EARLY, the case playing on her mind. Her thoughts kept returning to her conversation with Ellen the night before. She struggled to understand how what appeared to be a hard-working family had come to harm. Ellen didn't have a bad word to say about them, which prompted Karen to call through to her team. She needed the night shift to look at each individual member of the family. Before turning in for the night, Ty had confirmed the two farms on either side of the Lawsons were owned by the Dixon family.

That, together with what Ellen had mentioned, piqued Karen's interest and prompted her to pay a visit to Pat Dixon, the owner of the farm. The route was familiar, since she'd travelled it several times, so she found the address easily. As she pulled in through the gates, she slowed her car to take in the surrounding view. It was expansive and on a completely different level than the Lawsons' or Wagstaffs'. They, in comparison, looked like small holiday camps, as large industrial units the size of football pitches loomed in front of Karen. She wasn't sure what she'd expected, but it certainly wasn't this. Intrigued, she followed the long driveway a few hundred yards before reaching a double-storey Portakabin with the sign above it announcing she had arrived at Dixon Holdings Limited.

Hardly sounds agricultural, Karen thought as she stepped from the car and took in her surroundings. Once she made her way towards the door, which displayed a reception sign above it, Karen paused, her mouth open in shock. To her right and between adjacent buildings, she saw larger industrial units. From her position, she counted eight. There were vast, single-storey steel fabricated units that extended for as far as the eye could see. It was like nothing she'd seen before. "What have you got in there?" she muttered.

After Karen stepped through the door to reception, a woman dressed in a white polo shirt with the Dixon Holdings Limited logo on the left breast greeted her.

Karen held up her warrant card. "I'm looking for Pat Dixon. He is expecting me."

The receptionist asked her to take a seat to one side, but Karen hadn't moved before the sound of heavy footsteps came from beyond reception and a man wearing a baseball cap appeared. He had a weathered face, crow lines around his eyes, thin, tightly pursed lips, and a silvery red beard. He, too, wore a matching T-shirt, grubby faded jeans, and walking boots.

"Dixon," the man offered, extending his hand. "Your office called earlier. What's up?"

The man's lack of politeness and his curt tone got Karen's back up. So much so that she didn't extend the courtesy of responding to his offer of a handshake. "I'm Detective

Chief Inspector Karen Heath. I'm investigating the fire at the Lawson farm."

"And?"

Karen formed a mental picture of this man. He hadn't expressed an ounce of sadness or shock for the loss of the Lawsons.

"I wonder what you can tell me about the Lawsons? I'm speaking to all the farmers in the area to build up a better picture of the family and their connections."

"Well, if you're asking me who murdered them, then I can't help you."

I never said that they were murdered, and we haven't released that detail to the public. So I wonder what made you think that?

Karen filed that away and continued. "How well did you know them?"

"Not very well. He got on with his business, and I got on with mine. We had two contrasting business models, so we had little reason to cross paths. Anything else?" Dixon replied, pulling at his phone from his back pocket and swiping his finger across the screen a few times before tucking it away again.

"Am I keeping you from something?" Karen asked.

Dixon shook his head. "I'm a very busy man. I'd love to help you with your enquiries, but I can't see how."

Karen looked around the office. Behind reception, there were four other desks occupied by staff. Two were typing, the other two were on the phones. She was too far away to make out their words, but further phones were ringing towards the back of the office somewhere. "Can you tell me more about your business?"

Dixon sighed and looked bored, as if he'd been asked to stay behind after class and do his homework. "I own a mega farm. Poultry. Two hundred and fifty thousand hens. Should be up to four hundred thousand by the end of the year. I've got more units being built on another site."

"Impressive." Karen nodded.

Dixon threw her a sarcastic smile. "It's just the beginning. The site down the road is going to be the beginnings of a mega dairy farm. Five hundred cows, growing to seven hundred and fifty. Zero grazed, so they're not allowed out into the field and are kept inside sheds. Means we don't need as much land wasted on grazing, and we get a better return per acre." As he spoke, his tone vibrated with his excitement. "Big business in the US. You watch, it's growing in popularity here. I want to make sure that I'm the pioneer of mega farms in the UK."

"And the welfare of animals doesn't bother you? Can't be much fun for the cows to be stuck indoors 24/7? Not to mention the milk is much healthier when it comes from grass fed cattle?"

Dixon shrugged. "Look, officer, they're not pets. They're assets. Nothing more, nothing less. They make me money. Moneyboxes on four legs. They're born, they produce milk, they die. When that happens, we replace them with fresh stock. No emotional or personal attachment to them. That's the best way."

What a tosser.

"When was the last time you saw anyone from the Lawson family?" Karen asked.

Dixon rolled his eyes. "No idea. Probably a few weeks ago. I was out front, and I saw Lawson's son drive past in his pickup with the trailer on the back with a couple of bales of hay. As I said, our paths don't cross. He stays out of my way, and I stay out of his."

"So, you didn't see eye to eye? Did you have run-ins with him in the past?" Karen probed.

"Not sure how you arrived at that conclusion," Dixon spat. "Going by your accent, you're not from around here. People in the agricultural business keep to themselves. I only mix with people connected to my business, or who can add value to my business. All the other farms round here work on a much lower level. I do not need to talk to them."

Taking joy in winding him up, Karen ignored his flippant comments. "Did you hear or see anything unusual on Saturday night going into Sunday morning? Anyone hanging around? Any cars or vans that drove past at an unusual hour of the night?"

"What am I? A lollipop lady?"

Karen ignored him and continued.

"Mr Dixon, where were you on Saturday night and the early hours of Sunday morning?"

Dixon straightened and pulled his shoulders back. "Am I a suspect? I don't like where you're going with this."

"I'm asking everyone in the local area where they were on the night of the fire. It's a standard question."

Dixon studied her for a moment before answering. "Finished my rounds about ten p.m. Back home. Did the admin and went to bed around midnight. My wife will confirm that, as she hates being woken."

"Have you come across anyone trespassing on your land in the last few days? Especially close to the boundary between yourselves and the Lawsons?"

"Nope." Dixon huffed.

"Is it a twenty-four-hour operation?"

Dixon nodded.

"What about your staff who work here overnight? Could any of them have seen or heard anything?"

"You'd have to ask them."

"Oh, don't worry, Mr Dixon, I intend to. Here's my card. If you think of anything, call me? Thank you for your help and time," Karen said before turning and walking away with a smile.

After escaping the annoying man, Karen jumped back in her car and headed back up the drive before turning right and driving past the Lawson farm. According to Ty, the next farm she would come to was also owned by Dixon. Karen spotted a sign a few hundred yards up the road. She indicated and pulled over to the side as soon as she found the entrance to the second farm that Dixon was talking about. The mega dairy.

Construction was well underway with large steel fabricated buildings being erected side by side. It looked grand and impressive. A few of the workers saw Karen's car blocking the entrance and stopped their work to look at her. She spotted one worker reaching for his phone as he pointed towards her and knew exactly who he'd be calling. Dixon had hemmed in the Lawson farm on both sides. As she started the car and pulled away, she wondered if the already frosty relationship between Dixon and the Lawsons had escalated.

16

KAREN REVIEWED her notes whilst checking the whiteboard for any new information added by her officers as she waited for them to come together for another update. Murmured conversations and a few laughs rippled around her as the team shared the trials and tribulations of everyday life. She picked up on a conversation by one of her officers, Delia, who moaned about running late because her little daughter had a summer cold and snotted all over her work top as she dressed for work this morning. "She had more slime coming out of her nose than a walking zombie," Delia remarked, much to the amusement of her colleagues.

After the side conversations died down, Karen turned to face her team. "Morning everyone. I thought it would be good to have a quick update. It's rare that we deal with multiple victims in the same case, so I'd like for us to move on this swiftly. How did we get on with the search of the immediate area?"

Jade stepped in first. "We've had a search team scouring the gardens, barns, and the immediate field behind the farmhouse. We found a few items of interest. A couple of discarded dirty clothes stuffed in a carrier bag by the back door, a screwdriver, a few jackets and T-shirts tossed around the barns, and several empty chemical containers. We have secured them for analysis, but we're talking about a farm here. I'd imagine that those kinds of things are scattered around most farms."

Karen agreed. Any one of the Lawsons could have dropped a screwdriver from their back pocket. Most farms used an assortment of industrial chemicals not found in a domestic setting. It bothered Karen. If they had found such items near to a domestic house fire, they may have been significant discoveries, but she doubted these items carried the same significance.

Karen turned to Belinda. "Bel, any joy with the CCTV?"

Belinda looked up from her notes and gave Karen a small, warm smile. With her rounded face, and her full cheeks, Bel reminded Karen of a chipmunk, though she hadn't had the balls to tell her for fear of offending her. But whenever Belinda laughed, she reminded Karen of the cartoon characters from *Alvin and the Chipmunks*.

"We didn't find any further CCTV cameras on the property other than the ones we'd found in the barns and the sheds. The fire unfortunately destroyed the recorder. It was situated upstairs in the study. We might retrieve the hard drive data with the help of the high-tech unit. I'll chase that up for you."

"That would be helpful. Thanks." Karen stepped to one side and looked at the profile pictures of the Lawson family. "Our first question was why didn't the family wake up and escape? I now believe that they were intoxicated when they went to bed. The theory carries more strength because Ellen, the herdsperson, mentioned the Lawsons had won a major contract with a chain of supermarkets to supply them with cheese from the farm."

"They were celebrating. Hence all the wine bottles," an officer remarked.

Karen nodded. "Exactly. The first post-mortem revealed soot in the airways and nasal passages. They died from smoke inhalation. My guess is that all six victims will show the same outcome. But I don't know if the intention was to scare them or cause harm."

"But we still don't know if they were all the intended victims or just one of them," the officer added.

"That's true. And we may never know," Karen replied with a shrug. "We have one victim who tried to escape. My guess is that he hadn't drunk as much but was too unwell or weak to open the windows, let alone escape because of mobility issues."

"I looked at the post-mortem report. Obviously, there weren't any distinguishable features because of the state of the remains. Any idea on how we are going to confirm their identities?" Ned asked.

"Dental records if the teeth are intact. Izzy is taking care of that. Forensics may be able to carry out DNA analysis if Izzy can recover deep tissue matter and blood, but most body fluids evaporate when the victim has been burnt this badly. There may also be hair fibres in the farm vehicles and on the items of clothing found around the barns." The enormity of the investigation wasn't lost on Karen. DNA analysis was a key tool in the identification of suspects and victims in modern-day policing. With the remains of the victims being badly burnt, it made the task of the forensic team more challenging.

"I have no news about the type of accelerant used, nor the tox reports on the first victim," Karen said. "As soon as I have them, they'll go on the system." She moved over towards the map that was attached to another whiteboard. A red pin had been placed over the Lawson farm. Karen pointed towards two blue pins sat either side of the red one. "These two farms belong to Pat Dixon. I had the unfortunate pleasure of meeting with him. Dixon is a businessman. Not a farmer. He's not going to win any awards for personality of the year. Rude and abrasive, he saw and heard nothing even though his farms sit either side."

"If you look on the map, his farms look massive compared to the Lawsons'," Ty remarked.

"They are. He operates what he referred to as a mega farm. Can someone look into that and get back to me? I need the summary, not chapter and verse. The Lawsons were hemmed in on both sides. It makes me wonder if Dixon had his eye on their farm. It could be a motive."

A few of her officers made notes as they formulated their own theories.

"John Lawson has a brother in Wales, Daniel. Track him down. Be gentle when you break the news," Karen said, turning towards Jade.

Jade gave her the thumbs up. "We've not been able to find the vehicle details for the car that ran Marcus and Natasha off the road. I thought it would be useful to put up a sign on the road asking for information. Perhaps even extending the search for CCTV a few miles in either direction?"

Karen nodded her approval and asked Jade to push forward with that as a matter of urgency before opening up the floor to any other information from her officers.

A support officer waved her pen in the air to catch Karen's attention.

Karen spun on her heels towards Rozana, a retired police officer who had come back in a civilian capacity in part because she still loved the job. Being part of a team of Asian officers, she and her colleagues were a vital conduit towards building better relationships between the police and Asian communities. Rozana devoted much of her time coming together with groups created to assist and support Muslim women who were regularly under-represented in the police service, and were also the target of strict male-dominated Asian communities who regarded women as second-class citizens.

Rozana had been drafted in as Karen's team swelled to handle the investigation. "What have you got, Rozana?" Karen asked.

"Karen, we've been speaking to a few locals. Again, no one had a bad word to say about the Lawsons. I checked their financial records as well. They recently took on twelve grand of debt to purchase new equipment for the farm. The profit and loss accounts looked healthy, and the bank didn't see them as a high-risk client. They went through a period a few years back when their income dropped significantly, but they appeared to bounce back."

Rozana checked it was okay to continue as Karen added those notes to the whiteboard. "The bank had been in discussions with the Lawsons about a revised projection for their business based on a new dairy contract being awarded to them. That must be the contract for the cheese that you mentioned earlier?"

"Okay, thanks. I think that's all for the moment, folks. Shout if you uncover anything." Karen tapped the tip of the marker pen on her chin as she thought things through. She headed over towards Ty's direction and leant over his desk. "You okay after yesterday?" she asked in a hushed tone.

Ty smiled at her. A soft warmth filled his eyes, a sign of appreciation. He offered a small nod. "I'm okay. I processed it last night. The first one was always going to be the hardest. But thanks. Thanks for thinking of me."

Karen gave a small wink and nudged him in the arm. "My pleasure. Always here for you. I was more worried about you throwing up on my shoes than anything else."

Ty laughed as Karen walked off.

17

KAREN DROPPED into the chair behind her desk and thought about the case. Through the glass front of her office, she watched her team filtering back to their desks, a couple of them hanging around and discussing their own theories and the next steps. She felt an enormous sense of pride as she watched them. It was a good team. There were no egos, and none of the bullshit attitude that she had witnessed so much of in London. Everything flowed smoothly, like a well-oiled machine. Team members were more than willing to help and support each other without a second thought. She loved working with all of them.

Karen held a particular fondness for Belinda, Ty, and Ed. Perhaps because they were the first officers she'd been introduced to, but they had also embraced Jade's arrival with open arms. She was the first to admit that she'd been nervous about tearing Jade away from her life in London to bring her up here. But it seemed to have paid off. Jade was loving her job. The team seemed to work well under her, and there was a potential budding romance brewing between Jade and James. Even the first initials matched, which tickled Karen.

Her thoughts turned towards the case again as she switched on her computer and wiggled her mouse to wake up the screen. She knew this case was going to be a challenging one. With evidence thin on the ground, and no witnesses or CCTV, she'd have to work hard to crack this case. The post-mortems would continue today, and she didn't envy Izzy's task.

Karen agreed to send Ed and Preet on her behalf. It wasn't a pleasant thing for either of them to experience, but some aspects of policing were harsh, and officers needed a thick skin to deal with them. She knew Ed had been to post-mortems before, but Preet hadn't attended many, so this would be a good test for her. Ideally, best practice always recommended that two officers needed to be present during a post-mortem in case one of them passed out. Logistically, that wasn't always possible, and Karen had lost count of the number of occasions where she had attended a post-mortem on her own.

Karen knew nothing about farming, the intricacies, the day-to-day work, the rivalries, nor the history that appeared to be deeply set within most farming families. As she scrolled through her emails, she speculated on the motive. There was nothing concrete to go on so far, just loads of hunches. It may have been an act of jealousy or revenge. Did John Lawson settle an unknown debt with his life? Karen pursed her lips. It may not have even been connected to John Lawson. She wondered if any of his children were implicated. Had they done something wrong? Her thoughts turned towards his wife. Had she been involved in an illicit affair that turned sour? The spurned lover exacting revenge.

There were so many questions, and she was in no position to rule any of them out. Karen logged into Facebook and Instagram before searching out the social media profiles for the family and the farm. She scanned a few posts about farmers' events taking place locally, and the opening hours and new products on offer in their farm shop. Any comments attached to those posts appeared favourable as Karen scrolled down the page.

Karen flicked over to Instagram, finding hundreds of photos posted by various members of the family. It appeared to be a much more active page than the Facebook one. Pictures of the dairy cattle, various members of the family sitting on tractors, the milking parlour, the herd being milked, and lots of smiling faces. *They looked a happy bunch*, Karen thought. The pictures of John's children matched those on the whiteboard. They appeared a hard-working farming family.

She stopped scrolling at the pictures of John Lawson and his wife standing close together holding what appeared to be a framed award between them. Karen scrolled down the page to discover similar pictures. Some contained framed awards, others featured John holding a platter of large cheese wedges, and a few were taken inside what appeared to be a cold room where blocks of cheese were stacked on shelves.

They were certainly an industrious family, Karen thought as she leant back in her chair and rocked back and forth. Was the arson attack an attempt to knock out the competition?

The most recent pictures interested her most. Posted Saturday night, the timestamp saying eight forty-two p.m., pictures of them all standing side by side, their wine glasses held high in celebration as they posed for a family photograph. Karen tapped her fingers on the table as she mulled over the information. If the timestamp was correct, they were still alive before nine p.m. They tragically lost their lives within a four-hour window of when the fire was started.

18

"KAREN, HAVE YOU GOT A MINUTE?" Jade asked, loitering in her doorway.

"I've always got a minute for you. Park your arse on that chair." Karen raised her arms and afforded herself a nice stretch before shaking her head and getting comfortable again. "These chairs are so bloody comfortable that I feel like falling asleep if I sit here too long."

"You are management, after all. They always push out the budget for management. Our chairs aren't as comfortable," Jade replied, shuffling in the seat opposite Karen.

"What's up?"

"A few things. The team has been doing a bit of online research, and they've found a few news articles posted yesterday about the tragic fire at the Lawson farm. The articles are nicely written and complimentary. I don't get it." Jade sighed. "No one has a bad word to say about them. They've not put a foot wrong and yet someone wanted one or all of them dead." Jade passed across a few printouts of news articles.

Karen leant forward and scanned them. "They even congratulate the Lawsons on their recent contract," she said as she ran her finger down each page. "Jealousy?" Karen suggested, looking up at Jade, who did nothing but shrug.

Karen noted down the name of the reporter who'd published the piece and added it to her list of people to call. Karen was about to continue when her mobile rang. She checked the screen but didn't recognise the number.

"DCI Karen Heath here."

"Oh, hi. It's Ellen here. I just wanted to give you a quick call to say that I found Bonnie."

Karen's face lit up as a big smile radiated from her. "Oh. That's fantastic. Where did you find her?"

"I found her burrowed deep in between two big bales of hay at the back of the hay barn. I doubt she had moved since the fire. She was so thirsty and weak. Poor girl was petrified."

Karen's heart fluttered in sadness. She couldn't imagine how terrified the dog was upon seeing the fire. Her officers searching the barn hadn't helped either.

"I'll take her back with me. She knows me well enough. Every time I'm on the Lawson farm, Bonnie follows me around. It makes sense for her to stay with someone she knows."

Karen agreed with Ellen and thanked her for calling before hanging up.

"That's great news," Jade said. "If only dogs could talk. There's a good chance she saw the perp start the fire."

"Bloody shame. It would save us a stack of time."

"Anyway, I've contacted Daniel, John's brother. He's coming down later today and will meet you tomorrow at the farmhouse if that's okay?"

"How did he take the news?" Karen asked.

"Local police had first spoken to him on our behalf and then I called. He didn't say anything for what felt like a few minutes. I guess he thought he was dreaming or had misheard. He stuttered out his reply that he would sort himself out and make his way over."

"Okay, thanks, Jade."

"There's one other thing. The Lawsons' solicitor wants a quick word. Here's his number. Can you bell him now?" Jade asked, handing Karen a yellow Post-it.

Karen took the number and punched it into her desk phone before putting the call on loudspeaker. Philip Foster answered, introducing himself in a clean London accent.

"Mr Foster, I'm Detective Chief Inspector Karen Heath from York police. I understand you wanted a quick word with me?"

"Detective Chief Inspector, thank you for returning my call so quickly. I'm one of the solicitors at Chadwick and Masters law firm based here in York. I handle all the legal affairs for the Lawson family. I understand that you're dealing with their tragic deaths."

"I am, Mr Masters."

"Philip is fine. I was both saddened and shocked by the news that the whole family had lost their lives in such an awful way. Anyway, I wanted to let you know I will still be handling their legal affairs in accordance with John Lawson's will in due course."

"Had legal provision been made for the farm to be taken care of?" Karen asked.

There was a brief pause at the end of the line. "Well, there lies the problem. John expressed that he would hand the farm down to his three children, and they would each own a third share. Unfortunately, with them passing too, I'll be reaching out to his next of kin."

Karen pointed out that Daniel, John's brother, would arrive later today and that it would be sensible for Philip to reach out to him.

"I know this might border on client confidentiality, Philip, but I'm dealing with a multiple murder investigation. Do you know of any threats of violence towards any member of the family?"

"I'm sorry, DCI. I'm unaware of such things. Nothing was brought to my attention."

"Did John sound concerned or looked worried when you last met him?"

"There was nothing in the tone of his voice to suggest that. We conducted most of our work over the phone. I last saw him in person fourteen months ago."

"Right. Okay, that's helpful. If I need to run anything by you again, is it okay for me to call you on this number?" Karen asked.

"Of course. I'd be happy to help in any way that I can. There is one other thing that might be of use to you. I'm not sure if you are aware of his neighbour. Pat Dixon."

Karen rolled her eyes in Jade's direction. "Yes, I am. I visited him as part of my investigations."

"Ah, that's helpful. Pat Dixon offered to buy out John's farm twice in the past three years. John made me aware of both offers before rejecting them."

"What was John's opinion of the offers?"

"Well, they were very healthy. Above market value on both occasions. Money wasn't a problem as far as Mr Dixon was concerned. He wanted John's farm and would pay over the odds for it."

Karen raised a brow as she and Jade exchanged looks of curiosity.

"Did John consider the offers at all?"

"Other than sharing the offers with me, John said he had no interest at all in selling the family business and had made that emphatically clear to Pat Dixon. It was going to stay a *traditional* family business. Those were his exact words to both me and Pat Dixon."

"Do you think that left any animosity between the pair?" Karen probed.

"Perhaps animosity on John's side. After rejecting the first offer, he was a little frustrated that seventeen months later, Pat Dixon pestered him again about selling. That's all I know, but I thought it would be helpful to share that with you."

"Philip, thank you for your call. It's been insightful. I really appreciate your time."

Karen hung up and stared at Jade for a few moments. "Well. I wasn't expecting that. Can you do a bit more digging on Dixon for me? I think I need to pay him another visit."

19

Once Karen arrived at the Dixon farm, she followed the directions given to her by the receptionist. The woman promised she would radio ahead to let Mr Dixon know to keep an eye out for her. With that done, she stepped back outside. The double-storey Portakabin disappeared from view as she followed the signposts to unit five. It was like a maze. There were large steel fabricated buildings in every direction. She figured each one must be at least a hundred metres long, if not longer, and about fifty metres wide. Karen had never seen anything like this. If this was farming, then it was on an industrial scale and far beyond what she had ever imagined.

The nearer she got to the unit, the more she noticed an unpleasant smell surrounding her. There were ventilation chimneys built into the roof of each unit emitting a horrible, sweet, sickly smell that was overpowering. She placed her hand over her mouth and nose to shield her from the worst of it.

A bleeping noise somewhere off to her left grew louder. The source became apparent when a large forty-foot articulated lorry came into view, reversing alongside a perimeter fence. An industrial unit on the flatbed was the height of a double-decker bus. In Karen's opinion, it resembled some kind of generator, though she lacked technical understanding to know for certain. She considered why Dixon would need something like this and what would it be used for.

Dixon's voice reached her before he did as he shouted at someone or something. When she turned the corner, Dixon loomed up ahead, pacing up and down, barking into his walkie-talkie. Something about dickheads and supply chain issues pierced Karen's eardrums. When Dixon spotted her, the obnoxious man tucked the walkie-talkie back into its holster on his belt.

"DCI Heath. Back so soon. What is it this time?" Dixon asked, pulling out his phone and swiping his finger across the screen a few times in search of something.

"I was passing on the way to the Wagstaff farm. I thought I'd check in on the Lawsons' herd they're looking after."

"I didn't know that animal welfare checks were on your job description?" he said with a snigger.

Karen suppressed a smirk. "They're not. I have other questions that I'd like to ask Charles Wagstaff, so you were on my way."

"You thinking of buying their herd?" he laughed as he turned his back on her and began walking off.

Karen raised a brow and tutted as she followed behind him. "I noticed a large lorry reversing back there. What is it carrying?"

"An industrial incinerator. DEFRA approved. A backup for burning dead carcasses for when we can't get them collected quick enough. I'll show you what we do with them?"

"What's that smell?"

Dixon sniffed the air and laughed. "You get used to it after a while. I can hardly smell it. It's a mixture of the bedding, chicken droppings, and other things that I won't go into. I'll take you into one shed if you want?" he offered.

Karen ignored the offer. "I heard you made two offers for the Lawson farm over the last three years. Rejected both times."

Dixon stopped, his back still to Karen. A few seconds passed before he slowly turned and rested his hands on his hips. "And?"

"Well, it looks like you are a successful and industrious man. You like to do things on a bigger scale than most people around here. I wondered if it pissed you off?"

"What? Enough to kill an entire family?" he sarcastically said.

"I didn't say that at all." Karen looked around and gestured with her hand. "You're a businessman, not a farmer. I get that. My guess is that you are looking to snap up as much land as you can. Earlier on this morning, you said you wanted to be one of the biggest mega farms in the UK. In order to do that, you'd need a lot more land."

Dixon looked down for a moment before folding his arms across his chest and looking up. "Yes, I offered to buy his farm twice. I offered good money. More than they could ever get if they sold it on the open market. It was a good deal. If I could buy his farm, I'd be able to merge this place with his, and my other farm."

"Right, I see." Karen pursed her lips and nodded, pretending as if she had only just joined the dots and figured out his strategy. "You wanted to merge all three farms and create a mega mega farm!" She smiled as she snapped her fingers.

"Something like that."

"Did it piss you off that they rejected your offer... twice?"

"No. DCI, understand that I run a business. They rejected the couple of offers I made. Eventually, I would have made them an offer which they would have accepted. It could have been this year, next year, five years' time, or even ten years'. It's a tough time out there for farmers. Subsidies are being squeezed, margins are tighter, feed prices are going up, produce prices are going down, exports cost more... Shall I go on? Everyone... reaches a breaking point. I was in no hurry. I would have had that farm eventually."

Dixon's assessment was cold and hard. Stripped of emotion or understanding. "Did John Lawson ever tell you to back off and leave him and his farm alone?" Karen asked.

Dixon levelled his eyes at Karen. "No."

"Okay, Mr Dixon. That's all for now. I'll let you get on. Thanks for your time."

"Come again, DCI. It's been a hoot." Dixon turned on his heel and marched towards the unit before throwing the door open and striding inside.

The crescendo of thousands of chickens clucking over-whelmed Karen's senses as she walked away.

20

THE WAGSTAFF FARM offered a relaxed vibe as Karen drove through the gates and headed towards an area of hard-standing close to the barns. She left her car and heard the familiar sound of cows echoing around her. Slipping on her welly boots, Karen set off in search of Ellen and found her shifting heavy bags of feed from the back of her jeep and dropping them by the side of a storage unit.

"Ellen, bet that keeps you fit," Karen said as she paused by the jeep and spotted a black and white collie further across the yard, head down, sniffing the ground.

Ellen wiped the sweat from her brow with the back of her hand. "It definitely does in this heat. Phew. I'm knackered already," Ellen replied, joining Karen and grabbing a bottle of water from her cab. "Fancy a walk? I need to check on the herd."

Karen smiled and nodded, telling Ellen to lead the way. "Is that Bonnie?"

"Yes. She's a good girl. Bonnie... let's go," Ellen shouted before whistling to get Bonnie's attention.

"How is she?"

"I guess she's okay. Follows me around everywhere. Lays by my feet in the evenings. I'm sure she's missing John and the family, but it's the least I can do for them."

Ellen opened a metal gate and stepped through with Bonnie and Karen before closing it behind them. They traipsed through the field and through another gate which opened up into a much larger field, twice the size of the one they had just left. Off in the distance, a large herd of about thirty cows huddled in a group grazing on the grass.

Karen glanced around and smelt the freshness. A subtle odour of freshly cut grass hung in the air. Other than the occasional moo and snort, silence surrounded her. It felt like a million miles from London. There was a gentleness and freedom that felt refreshingly relaxing. She stepped around the cowpats that littered the ground, but she was getting used to them. Karen noticed her shoulders drop and serenity wash over her. She had never taken herself as a country girl but having been out in the rural landscape for the past few days, she could see its attraction. Karen could imagine herself one day living in a small country cottage, enjoying her retirement and embracing walks in this vast openness.

Bonnie raced up and down the field, bouncing with joy and chasing a ball that Ellen kept throwing for her.

"I do envy your lifestyle, Ellen. Being outdoors all the time beats being stuck behind a desk," Karen remarked as she scanned the horizon.

Ellen laughed. "It's not all glamorous. Especially when you're waking up at three a.m. for milking the girls in the middle of winter or when you pull an all-nighter calving in spring."

"I see your point. But then again, I've lost count of the number of times I've been woken during the night and called out to a murder scene. The stuff I've seen would put you off your cornflakes."

"Rather you than me," Ellen replied, throwing the ball again.

"I visited Dixon on the way here. I found out he'd tried to buy the Lawson farm on two occasions that we know of. What do you make of him?"

"Honestly?" Ellen asked.

"Go for it."

"He's rough and abrasive. I know he doesn't take rejection too well. Dixon is a competitive businessman, plain and simple. He's not a farmer with a passion for farming." Ellen waved her hand in front of her. "I see this land as not only my workplace, but as a piece of our history as a country. We have worked this land for hundreds of years. Generations of families have tended to this land. Children have grown up with this as their back garden. We've cultivated the land. We've grown produce. We've looked after the wildlife that call this their home and created an income for families."

Karen loved the passion and pride that Ellen exuded as each word left her lips. She had sensed none of that in her conversations with Dixon.

"It means a lot to you, doesn't it?" Karen questioned.

"Does it show?" Ellen smiled.

"Just a tad."

Ellen's forehead crinkled. "Dixon is motivated by profit. He tried to poach me twice. He wanted me to work for him. Big salary. Big promises. He seems to think everyone has a price."

Karen and Ellen stopped by a gate at the far end of the field and leant up against it. There was plenty of warmth in the air. The sun was edging closer to the treeline on the horizon. Birdsong floated around them.

"Why didn't you take up his offer?" Karen asked.

"I hate to say it, but I don't like the man. I don't like his approach to business, and I don't like his demeanour. He's a bit too friendly sometimes. Almost as if his words mean one thing, but looking into his eyes, he has other things on his mind as he looks me up and down. I get the feeling that there's a real ruthless streak in him. I guess he would need that with the type of business he's running. It takes a lot of guts and balls to do what he's doing. I doubt he will let anyone stand in his way. At least not for long."

Karen watched as Bonnie charged around the field, full of energy and joy. She still wondered what Bonnie had silently observed. In her mind, Bonnie may have been the only witness to what unfolded at the Lawsons'.

Karen and Ellen headed back towards the barns as the evening milking round approached. It would soon be time to bring the herd in. As if already knowing, the herd ambled across the field in the direction the humans were heading.

"How did news of the contract go down with the surrounding farms?" Karen asked.

"As far as I know, it was well received. I think a few of the farmers were a tad envious, but in a nice way. It's a hard life on the farm. Picking up awards or contracts for cheese or prized beef, or even the best turkeys, goes down really well. It gives everyone hope, and that's important in these times." Ellen pulled the scrunchie from her hair before reapplying it to a fresh ponytail.

"Thanks for your time, Ellen. It's been helpful. I'll let you get on."

"No worries. If you ever need to get away from work for a few hours to clear your head, you know where to come."

"I'll take you up on that."

21

KAREN LEANT BACK in her office chair and yawned. With the late shift continuing to do a background trawl of the Lawsons' business and with the addition of Pat Dixon to their searches, Karen knew the team had their hands full. It had been a long day and though she had wanted to go home, her visit to Dixon played on her mind. Maybe he was nothing more than an egotistical businessman driven by profit, but there was something about him that didn't sit easily with Karen.

She opened the Google page on her desktop and punched in mega farms. She scrolled through a few pages and then refined her search criteria. As her eyes scanned through pages of information, it soon became clear to Karen that the mega farm concept had first appeared in the US but had gained popularity in the UK in recent times. Jotting down a few points on a pad of paper, Karen uncovered the startling fact that more than one thousand mega farms operated in the UK.

No wonder Pat Dixon is so keen to expand his business, she thought.

Karen's eyes narrowed as she scanned the details. The growth of such farms hadn't come without controversy. People had raised multiple concerns about animal welfare and air pollution in the surrounding areas of each farm and its impact on local wildlife. High concentrations of ammonia and other nitrogen-based emissions had caused direct damage to lichens, mosses and other plants, including bleaching and discolouration.

The more Karen read, the more concerned she became. Mega farms caused long-term damage to flora and fauna, and with local protests on the rise, planning permission for such large-scale intensive farming operations were being met with huge opposition.

There was a distinct possibility that the Lawsons had vigorously opposed any attempts by Dixon to buy their farm, and in revenge, Dixon had taken them out of the equation. It was just a hypothesis in Karen's mind, but the more she thought about it, the more credible it felt as she continued to discover even more articles online.

"Now this is interesting," she muttered.

One article in particular Karen stumbled upon highlighted that following an undercover investigation by a local newspaper in Wales, most of these farms had gone unnoticed, despite their size and the controversy surrounding them, in part because many farmers had expanded existing facilities rather than seeking new sites. That would explain why Dixon was after the Lawson farm. The article said that mega farms were pushing smaller farmers out of business, leading to the takeover of the countryside by larger agribusinesses, with the loss of traditional family-run farms. Her conversation with the Lawsons' solicitor sprung to mind.

"You're late?" Jade said, poking her head around the open door.

"Yes, doing a bit of research on mega farms. I know the team is looking into it anyway, but I had an itch that needed a scratch."

"I'm sure there's a cream for that." Jade winked.

"Ha ha, very funny."

"Daniel Lawson will be at the farm tomorrow at nine a.m."

"Great. Thanks for arranging that, Jade."

"Find anything interesting?" Jade asked, throwing a nod towards Karen's monitor.

Karen nodded. "Did you know that seven out of ten of the largest mega farms in the UK are poultry farms? And that they house more than one million birds, with the biggest two out of those seven capable of holding between one point five and one point seven million birds." Karen's eyes widened as she processed that figure. "Can you imagine the size of those farms? And, going by the smell that I noticed on Dixon's farm, and it's nowhere as big as these, I can't imagine the smell that comes from such places."

Karen took a few moments to share what she had found with Jade, including the fact that the biggest pig farm in the UK held twenty-three thousand pigs.

"But that's not farming." Jade remarked. "Not even close to how I expected farming to be."

Karen shrugged. "I know. It's taken the *traditional* out of farming. It's all about profit now. These farms are getting a bit of heat. That's why from a cost and efficiency point of view, most farmers and large food companies have expanded existing facilities and farms, so they're going under the radar of local opposition."

"Cheeky buggers. But I guess the demand is there in the first place, otherwise we wouldn't have these mega farms?" Jade said, signalling air quotes when she mentioned mega farms. "Is that enough of a motive to kill? Do you reckon Dixon has it in him?"

"I'm not sure to be honest. He certainly comes across as being ruthless in business. I can't imagine many people enjoy crossing him. If the Lawsons continued to object to selling their farm to him, even with an inflated price tag, then they put a massive dent into his business plans. That could be enough..."

Jade's brows knit together. "We don't have enough to pull his chain at the moment. He's squeaky clean. With so much at stake, he would cover his tracks very well. I can't imagine him getting his hands dirty."

"He may have a few dodgy connections that could do the dirty work for him, Jade. I wouldn't put it past him."

"Fair point. Anyway, I'm off now. I'm meeting James for coffee and biscuits," Jade said, the corners of her mouth tugging upward.

Karen laughed. "Coffee and biscuits? You sound like an old couple. You need to head out for a tequila night?"

"James isn't a big drinker. It wouldn't be a fun night if I was knocking back tequila slammers, and he was on OJ."

Karen held her hand over her mouth as she stifled a yawn. "Sorry. I'm knackered. Enjoy your evening and I'll see you tomorrow."

Jade pulled her phone out and sauntered off, leaving Karen to look around her office. She hated to admit it to herself, but with the minimalistic and modern decor, she could sit here for hours. It wasn't like the dark, dingy, worn office spaces that she had spent so much time in back in London. Karen logged off and grabbed her belongings before calling it a night, too. Then she fished her phone out of her bag and dialled Zac's number.

"Hey you, you okay?" Karen asked as soon as Zac answered.

"All good here. I'm nagging Summer to get on with her homework, but she's being a pain in the proverbial."

"I heard that, Dad," came another voice down the line, which made Karen laugh.

"Sounds like you've got your hands full. I'm heading home now. I'm shattered. A shower, sandwich and bed for me, in that order. Is it okay if I come over tomorrow evening for dinner?"

"Of course, what do you fancy?" Zac asked.

"Now that's a loaded question," Karen teased.

"You're terrible. I meant to eat."

"Still a loaded question!" Karen chuckled to herself.

"Whatever. Sometimes having a sensible conversation with you is like pulling teeth. Come over whenever you want and we will figure out what to do… food wise."

"Okay. I'll call you as I'm heading over. Enjoy the rest of your evening. And say hi to Summer for me." Karen hung up and headed for her car.

22

KAREN EASED her car through the gates of the Lawson farm and pulled over on the left. She squinted as the morning sun streamed in through her windscreen. The day hadn't even started yet, but it was already getting warm. The forecasters had said that temperatures could peak at a high of twenty-nine degrees today. With weather like that, she'd much rather be lying in a garden with a good book and plenty of sun lotion.

Turning to her right, she saw the solemn figure of a man, hands stuffed deep in the pockets of his sleeveless gilet. A blue and white check shirt and faded jeans finished the classic farmer's outfit. With his back to her, he remained motionless, staring up at the boarded farmhouse, black soot trails snaking up the once white exterior. He cut a lonely figure. A man lost deep in thought.

Karen left the car and walked over to him. It seemed a shame to disturb him in his moment of grief. "Daniel? Daniel Lawson?" Karen asked as she came alongside him.

The man glanced across and nodded once before returning his gaze to the ruined building.

"I'm DCI Karen Heath of York police."

Karen joined him as she took in the sight. It was nothing more than a hollow shell of what once was a family home. Much of the roof structure had caved in. A few blackened timber struts poked through like an exposed ribcage. Silence surrounded them. None of the familiar sounds of everyday farming life. No cows. No tractors rumbling along. No dog barking. Nothing, not even a breeze.

"I'm sorry for your loss. My condolences to you and the rest of your family."

Daniel stared ahead and sniffed. "That was my family. They're all gone."

"I know. I can't understand how you might be feeling. But we are doing everything we can to find out what happened here."

"Arson, right?" Daniel mumbled, his lips hardly parting.

"Yes," Karen replied as she studied the man. He bore similarities to the pictures that she had of John and William Lawson. Though Daniel was much heavier, with a bald head and softer features, she felt they all had the same eyes, nose, and mouth.

Daniel remained rooted to the spot, his eyes moving from one window to another. "John was a proud man. He'd built all this up himself after Dad fell ill. We were all proud of him. He wanted to push the business forward. Farming was his passion... It was his life. He couldn't have done anything else. It was in his blood. All our blood. Things were getting tougher. It was harder to make a living. But that didn't deter him. He wanted to keep investing and growing. The new contract he'd secured…"

Daniel fell silent again as tears fell from his eyes like a dam opening its gate. His shoulders racked as he sobbed.

Karen placed a hand on his back and gave him a gentle rub. "I'm so sorry. Everyone I've spoken to so far didn't have a bad word to say about him. You *should* be proud of everything he achieved."

"Any idea who did this?" he asked through heavy sniffs.

"Not yet. It's an active investigation, so I can't say too much about it. I hope you understand. But as soon as I know more, I'll share it with you. You'll need to speak to Philip Foster, John's solicitor. He needs to talk to you about the farm."

"Okay," Daniel whispered.

Karen imagined that this wasn't the way he wanted to inherit his brother's farm. If it wasn't contested, the Lawson farm would go to Daniel. She speculated that if Daniel took over the farm, he'd demolish the farmhouse and start again. Perhaps picking a new location on the farm for a fresh start.

"There's never going to be an easy time to ask you, but did John or any members of his family tell you about any trouble that they were in? Debts? Arguments with neighbouring farms? Anything like that?" Karen asked.

Daniel looked across at Karen and seemed to falter as he was about to say something. He paused for a few seconds as he looked towards the farmhouse before returning his gaze in Karen's direction. "John told me on a few occasions he was scared of losing the farm. I tried to push him on why he felt that, but he never said. Something was bothering him. Every time I called, he seemed fine on the phone, but I could tell that he was distant as if something was on his mind."

"Do you know if he owed money to anyone? Perhaps someone lent him money?" Karen asked.

"I really don't know. I'm not sure he would have told me anyway because he knows I would have kicked his arse if he'd used a loan shark."

"Were they a strong family unit?"

"Yeah," Daniel nodded. "He'd brought up his kids properly. He wanted to make sure they understood family values and how the farm was a family business where everyone got involved. That was something important to him. Matt, Jess, and Rob did a grand job. The farm would have been safe in their hands."

"And you weren't aware of any threats against any of them?"

Daniel shook his head as his shoulders slumped.

"Okay, Daniel. Thanks for agreeing to meet me here today. I'll leave you in peace now, but here's my card. If you think of anything, call me."

Karen got back in her car and looked at Daniel. He hadn't moved. He stood staring at the farmhouse as she pulled away.

23

KAREN PUSHED through the doors of the SCU and made her way towards Ed. He was finishing up a call, so she dropped her bag beside his desk and popped over to see Jade. She leant in and spoke in a hushed tone. "How was bingo night for you? Did you hit the jackpot?" she teased.

Jade glared at Karen, mouth open. "Oh my God, Karen, you're terrible. We're not all looking to jump into bed at the first opportunity. It was coffee and biscuits. He was manning the desk at the outreach centre last night, so I popped in to keep him company for a couple of hours."

Karen winked. "Did you help him dunk his biscuit?" She nudged Jade with her elbow.

Jade nudged her back as they jostled like two teenage girls.

"Just teasing. Any updates?" Karen asked, straightening her back.

"The CCTV trawl for vehicles travelling along the lane continues. The signs are out by the roadside. We may get lucky." Jade scanned the case file. "No news on the CCTV hard drive, either. The high-tech team isn't hopeful. I spoke to them first thing this morning."

"I wasn't hopeful either, but it's worth a shot."

Jade tapped the end of her pen on the desk whilst she scrolled through her screen. "The forensics feedback has confirmed that the accelerant used to start the fire was petrol. They couldn't gather anything from the footprints. Too many boots on the ground contaminated and compromised any evidence." Jade narrowed her eyes as she scanned the fine print. "The same goes for the inside. Most of the evidence was destroyed by the fire and the water from the fire service. SOCO managed to lift a few prints from the wine bottles in the lounge. No match at the moment. And I'm not sure we'll get to compare them against the family either."

It wasn't the news Karen wanted to hear. Any scrap of forensic evidence would have helped her, but where fire and water were concerned, it destroyed everything usable like prints, hair and clothing fibres, blood samples, foot or hand prints, and anything else combustible.

"How did it go with Daniel Lawson this morning?" Jade asked.

Karen shook her head. "He was in bits. He's lost his whole family. There wasn't much I could say to console him."

Karen updated Jade on the things Daniel had said and how he was convinced that John was worried about losing the farm.

"And he didn't know what it was?" Jade asked.

"Nope. He just knew something was troubling his brother."

"You think it's anything to do with Dixon?"

Karen shrugged a shoulder. "Possibly. After everything Ellen said yesterday evening, the stuff I uncovered about mega farms, and another visit to Dixon, there is probable cause. Rejection. A desire to merge the farms to avoid planning objections. Huge profits. And I mean huge profits. Let's see what we uncover today," Karen said, noticing that Ed was free.

"How did it go yesterday, Ed?" Karen asked, perching on the end of his desk. Her eyes scanned his workspace. Meticulous, clean, neat and organised. Good old Ed. She scoured his desk for anything that appeared out of place to prove to herself that he wasn't perfect, perhaps a misplaced paper clip, the lid of a pen or a teacup stain. Nothing.

"The PM was tough, Karen. I think Preet found it harder than I did." He tapped his hand on the desk and said, "We tried to remain focused and objective. I don't think we can afford to get too emotional in such situations."

"Whatever works for you, Ed."

Ed gave her a summary of Izzy's findings, which mirrored those from the first post-mortem. He pointed out that they had recovered an engagement ring from the hand of one victim they believed to be Andrea, John Lawson's wife. The team had cross-referenced the ring with the images held on file for insurance purposes at the solicitors. They also discovered a metal hip joint whilst examining the second victim. With a serial number still intact, Izzy managed to confirm Grandad William Lawson as the recipient. He was the one found clutching the wheelchair after the fire.

"Okay, good. Hopefully Izzy can extract blood samples so we can do DNA analysis to formally identify the victims, but the engagement ring and hip joint will do for the moment. We can work with that."

Ed lifted his eyes to Karen's. "With that being the case, the last three victims have to be John and Andrea's children. Would you like me and Preet to attend again?"

Karen stepped back. "Are you okay with that? I'm more than happy for you to go. It would be helpful. Check with Preet that she's happy to attend again. If not, take Belinda or Ty."

"Ty's not up for it. I asked him as a backup. If Preet doesn't want to go, I'll check with Bel."

"Thanks, Ed. I appreciate it. If it ever gets too much today, call me. I'll draft someone in to take over, okay?"

"Sure."

Karen grabbed her bag and headed to her office. Dropping into her chair, she switched on her PC and jotted down a to-do list whilst she waited for her screen to kick into gear. The first thing on her mind was the news articles she'd seen about the Lawsons' fire and their awards. Karen tapped the number into her phone and waited. Her call was answered after a few rings.

"Henry Beavis, intrepid reporter, seeker of the truth, and fighter of justice for the common person."

Karen sat wide-eyed and smiled. "That's an introduction and a half. I wasn't expecting that. I'm DCI Karen Heath of York police."

Henry coughed and stuttered. "Um, yes. Well, um, if it's about the bald tyre your officer pulled me over for, I *am* getting it replaced. It's booked in at Kwik Fit tomorrow morning. I swear. I can send you the email confirmation."

Karen pursed her lips to avoid a laugh escaping. "Your secret is safe with me. I'm calling about a different matter, but make sure you turn up for your appointment tomorrow, otherwise the next call might not be as friendly," she teased.

"Sure. Yes. No problem. Anyway, how can I help?" His tone had switched from his jovial introduction to an air of seriousness.

"I'm the senior investigating officer overseeing the fire and tragic death of six members of the Lawson family. I've seen a couple of your articles covering the fire and their successes lately. I wondered if you could spare me some time. I'd like to meet with you, as I'm trying to build a better picture of the Lawson family and I'm not local to the area."

"Of course. No problem. When would you like to meet? My diary is pretty clear today."

"Are you free in the next hour? I could make my way over to you or we could meet for coffee in town?" Karen asked.

"Sounds great. Do you know Coffee Culture?" he asked.

"No, but it sounds interesting. I'll find it. Half an hour?"

"Great. See you then."

Karen hung up. *Interesting character*, she thought, as she scanned emails looking for anything urgent, before logging off and grabbing her bag.

24

HAVING DRIVEN around for ten minutes looking for a place to park, Karen headed off on foot to the address on Google Maps. She loved the narrow quirkiness of the city; it was like a warren of twisting streets where mock Tudor-fronted shops stood shoulder to shoulder with modern glass-fronted counterparts. When she looked ahead, the street had the strange visual effect of appearing to close in as buildings overhung the pavement in places. Antique shops, trendy restaurants, pubs and retail chains nestled amongst each other. *No wonder it draws local and international tourists. York has so much to offer*, she thought.

Coffee Culture had a grey frontage, which Karen almost missed as she breezed by. A quaint, cosy and informal setting, Karen noticed as she stepped through the door. It had the vibe of the young, trendy chic place. A mixture of tables, chairs and sofas offered visitors plenty of options. With a black fireplace and an array of framed photos and pictures on the walls, it might have been mistaken for someone's front lounge.

Karen looked around the coffee shop and noticed how narrow it became the further in she ventured. She spotted Henry sitting beside a window. She had checked his profile online before setting off, so she knew what he looked like. Tufty hair, gelled and spiked upward, a neatly trimmed beard, and always wearing a pair of sunglasses perching on his forehead. His picture didn't disappoint when she spotted the sunglasses.

"Henry Beavis?" Karen said, extending her hand.

Henry stood and shook her hand before offering her a seat. "Yes, what can I get you?"

Karen glanced over her shoulder and looked at the menu board. "I'll have a cappuccino if that's okay."

Henry shouted across to the man behind the counter, "Two cappuccinos, Chris."

Chris offered a nod before turning his back to get on with the order.

"Regular haunt for you?" she asked, noting the familiarity between the two men.

"You could say that. I went out with his sister for three years." Henry laughed.

Karen raised a brow. "Oh… that familiar."

Henry waved it away. "It's cool. It all ended good. There is no beef there. Anyway, how can I help?"

Chris brought over the coffees with a friendly smile. Karen waited for him to leave before speaking.

"As I mentioned on the phone, I'm the SIO dealing with the fire and loss of the Lawson family. I wanted your take on the family and to get a vibe about the local farming community. I know little about the area. I was based in London for most of my career. I've just moved here."

Henry looked down and shook his head. "Yeah, man. I was shocked by that. Really sad news. They were a well-liked family. They did well. I liked how they always wanted to innovate. They were branching out with the dairy products. Cheese in particular and, as you know, they'd recently snagged a nice little juicy contract. I think they were looking at producing their own yoghurt," he said with a shrug.

Karen made a few notes. "What do you know about Pat Dixon, the neighbouring farmer?"

Henry's face took on a tone of seriousness. "I'm not a fan. I'm much more about upholding local values. This area is about traditional farming. From what I know, local farmers aren't keen on his mega farm business."

"Did any of them ever have a face-to-face run-in with Dixon?"

Henry looked around and leant in as if he was about to share some top-secret information. "Is Dixon a suspect?"

As a reporter, Henry tried to steer the conversation. He was looking for the next juicy exclusive and a feather in his cap. Karen couldn't blame him for trying.

"No. I'm trying to build a better picture of the key players in the local area. From what I can gather, Pat Dixon seems to be one of them."

Henry played with his napkin. "You're not wrong there, DCI. From what I know, there have been a few secret meetings amongst local farmers opposed to the mega farm and

Dixon. I think nothing has been made public. But there's an undeniable undercurrent of anger and fear."

"Do you know of other farms affected by Dixon's mega farm?" Karen asked, taking a sip of her coffee and enjoying the mellow taste on her lips. It was creamy and smooth.

Henry nodded. "Find me a farm around here that hasn't been affected. If you've done your research, you'll know how damaging it is to the environment. To be honest, it's destroying local businesses and Dixon doesn't care who he rides roughshod over."

"Did you ever speak to any of the Lawson family in person?" Karen asked.

"I did. I'd interviewed John and his dad twice in the past few years. John showed me around the farm, and I could tell how passionate he was about his farm and farming. He was a farmer through and through. Do you know the cause of the fire?"

Karen smiled to herself. Henry was good at pivoting, a classic interviewing technique aimed at steering the conversation in the direction he preferred. With the press release imminent, she couldn't say anything.

"We should know soon. As soon as we do, a press release will go out."

"Come on, DCI. It would be between you and me. I'm doing you a favour, so help me out."

I can't blame him for trying. It was Karen's turn to pivot.

"What was the outcome of the secret meetings between local farmers?"

Henry rolled his eyes. He downed the rest of his cappuccino before continuing. "They said that Dixon was using aggressive tactics to intimidate local farmers."

Karen reared back a bit. "How so?"

"He was outbidding others at poultry auctions. Money is no object to him. He wants to be the biggest and best. He was also bidding too high on cattle and then pulling out before the lot sold, so farmers were ending up paying over the odds. Let me tell you, that went down like a sack of shit."

"Did anyone confront him about that?" Karen asked.

Henry's eyes widened. "Would you? The farmers around here haven't got the clout or the money to go up against him. He could ruin a business overnight. There were rumours he was spreading lies about other farmers to ruin their reputations."

"Like what?"

"Mistreatment of animals. Not settling bills with suppliers. Polluting the land and rivers."

The more she heard, the more Dixon worried her. There was far more to Dixon than she had realised. "Any of that true?"

"Your guess is as good as mine. I don't know the ins and outs of each farmer. My guess is no."

Karen asked a few more questions before thanking Henry for his time and rising to head for the door.

"DCI," Henry said as he stood up, "considering I've helped you out, how about an exclusive?"

"That's not how it works, Henry," Karen turned and replied.

"Of course, it is. I help you and you help me. It might be the start of a cracking working relationship…"

Karen let out a little chuckle. "Maybe, Henry. I'll think about it."

25

AFTER PARKING up at the station, Karen headed to the building that housed the forensic services unit. Having walked past Bart's team, she scooted along the narrow corridor before darting into the room that housed the high-tech unit.

Karen's phone chimed to alert her to an incoming message. She pulled it from her back pocket and, not recognising the number at once, swiped the screen. It was a message from Henry.

Have you thought about it?

He'd signed it with a smiley emoji.

Karen chuckled to herself. He was persistent. She'd give him that.

I'm still thinking about it.

After hitting send on her text, she stopped at the first desk, asking where Adil Choudhury was. A female officer jabbed her pen towards the back of the office. "You can't miss his desk. It's the untidiest."

"Thanks."

Karen weaved through the desks. Most of the officers sat in silence, their eyes glued to screens. She glimpsed a few monitors and didn't have a clue what the team was studying, but whatever it was looked complicated.

Towards the far end of the room, she spotted the untidiest desk. Laptops in clear evidence bags sat in a tall pile in one corner of the desk. Reams of paper sat in another pile, almost teetering on the edge at the other end. Two monitors shielded the person behind it. Walking around to the side, Karen peered around the two monitors.

"Adil?"

The young man tore his gaze away from the screen and blinked hard before smiling. "Yep, that's me."

On first impressions, Karen estimated he could pass as being an eighteen-year-old computer geek, though he was in his early thirties. A loose-fitting T-shirt hung from his bony frame, and his glasses sat perched on the tip of his nose.

"DCI Karen Heath. I know my team has been liaising with you about the recovered hard drive from the farmhouse fire. I badly need something from it. Anything. A face. A figure. Even a partial figure. It can't be that terribly screwed up, can it?"

"Karen. Like I said to your team, it suffered extensive fire damage. I'll show you what I've found already, but the recovery process is taking time." Adil held his hand up. "I know what you're gonna say. Time isn't on your side." He grabbed his mouse and clicked through a few screens before pulling up a video file.

Karen came around to his side of the desk and stood over his shoulder for a closer view of his screen.

Adil played the recording. The image was choppy in places, but one camera had captured an orange glow reflecting off the farm vehicles and sheds. Karen watched in silence for a minute before the tape stopped.

"Is that it?" she asked with a groan, crossing her arms across her chest.

He nodded. "That's it for that segment of footage. There was no movement. No figures. I'm sorry. I've recovered another clip." Adil played the second clip in his folder.

If the last clip was anything to go by, Karen had wasted a trip. She stared at the screen and saw nothing. Then a few seconds later she saw Bonnie racing into the barn and in between straw bales. Karen's heart flipped as she took a sharp intake of breath. *Poor Bonnie.* The footage continued for another minute before it stopped.

"I'm afraid that's all I've got. I'm still trying to see if I can recover anything else. But don't hold your breath."

Karen let out a deep sigh. "I'm not. Okay, thanks Adil. Any joy on the phones so far?"

"We have downloaded call data, phone logs and messages for three of the phones. They should be with your team by now. I believe they belong to the grandad, dad and mum. We're still working on the others."

Karen thanked Adil again before leaving and heading back to her office. She scanned her inbox and saw that they had uploaded the records to the case file. Further forensics updates had confirmed that one victim had been identified as John Lawson by his dental records. Karen scanned through the body of the email and cross-referenced it with the case file. They had the identities of John and the grandfather, William. A blood sample taken during one of the post-mortems had confirmed one victim as being Andrea, John's wife.

Karen sat back in her chair having read that the toxicology report on John Lawson had confirmed a high concentration of alcohol in a small blood sample recovered from his body. The concentration would have equalled someone being three times over the legal limit to drive. That gave Karen the theory John Lawson hadn't woken as the fire raged around him. He'd gone to bed drunk. His wife Andrea wasn't that far behind him in the toxicology report.

The report identified the presence of soot in both their lungs and throats. Though it was good to get those loose ends tied up, it didn't make her feel any better. She still needed to find out why they had suffered such horrific deaths. That question played on her mind the most and kept her awake at night. Karen had to assume that the post-mortem and toxicology reports on the other three victims would conclude with the same findings.

Karen picked up the phone and called Izzy.

"Karen, my lovely. How are you?" Izzy asked, her voice bright and breezy.

"Tired and frustrated. This case is dragging on a little. Anyway, I didn't call to moan. I wanted to say thank you for the time you've taken with our victims. It's not been an easy one for us, so I can only imagine how challenging it was for you."

"Aw, bless. Thank you, my lovely. It's nice to be appreciated. I won't lie. It's been bloody awful. I hate dealing with burnt corpses. Not only is it hard to look at them, but *so* difficult to get answers."

"I bet."

"Well, I've completed two more. One more to do this evening. Those two died of smoke inhalation. I managed to get samples, which I've sent off. But they're all following a similar pattern."

That news was a foregone conclusion in Karen's mind. If she was expecting to hear startling new evidence that opened a whole new line of enquiry, she was disappointed. On this occasion, Izzy wouldn't be her saviour.

"How have Ed and Preet been coping at your end?" Karen asked.

"It's not been easy for them. I think Preet has been more visibly moved than Ed. He seems to take the bloody thing in his stride. He didn't appear fazed at all. The man has a cast-iron gut. I'm not sure I can say the same about Preet. Bless her. Ed spoke, Preet jotted and took notes."

"I'll check in with her and make sure she's okay," Karen said before thanking Izzy and hanging up.

Karen had had enough of this long, drawn-out day. She made one last call to Daniel Lawson that went straight through to voicemail. She thought perhaps he was too distraught to talk, so left him a message asking if he was okay before she logged off and headed off to Zac's.

26

KAREN DRAGGED her weary body from the car and headed up the garden path before ringing on the doorbell. She waited for a moment and checked her phone. Karen tutted knowing she was already twenty minutes late.

"Coming," came Zac's voice from somewhere within the house, followed by footsteps before he opened the door and greeted her with a smile. "Sorry? Who are you? I'm not sure we've met before. I'm Zac, supposedly your boyfriend," he teased, holding his hand out for a handshake.

Karen shook her head in mock despair. "Some people just lack the ability to laugh at themselves. That's where I come in. It must be exhausting being in your mind," Karen replied, stepping into the hallway and dropping her bag by the bottom of the stairs.

Zac laughed, threw a tea towel over his shoulder, and pulled Karen into his arms, giving her a hug. "It's lucky you're my favourite person, or I'd be kicking you out the door again for being rude."

Karen wasn't listening to his one-liners as she wrapped her arms around his waist and pulled him in closer, savouring the moment. Zac tried to step back, but Karen pulled him in again. "Don't spoil the moment. I need this."

They stood silently for a few minutes, Karen enjoying the warmth of his embrace.

She eventually released her hold and smiled. "I'm bloody starving."

"You're always hungry," he said, leading her into the kitchen.

The smell of beef mince cooking away in a frying pan with Mexican spices filled the room. It felt warm and inviting, which only made Karen hungrier.

"Where's Summer?" Karen asked, standing by the back door and admiring the garden.

"Facetiming her mates upstairs. She will be down soon, and in the meantime, you can shred the lettuce and chop the tomatoes whilst I put the tacos in the oven."

They spent the next few minutes catching up on their days, with Karen telling Zac about her recent meetings with Pat Dixon and how he came across as such a tosser. He was fast becoming one of her least favourite people and with reason. The more she heard about Pat Dixon, the higher he climbed up her list of likely suspects, which only stood at one, Pat Dixon.

Between them, they threw out ideas for a motive and next steps for Karen. Zac offered nothing ground-breaking, but it was nice that he was taking a passionate interest, and Karen appreciated that. Frustration around her cases wasn't something she could discuss or even get off her chest if her partner was a civilian. Most couples in everyday life talked at great length about their jobs with their respective partners. Sharing their troubles, concerns, highlights and successes. Often, there was a mutual appreciation. But the role of a police officer often meant that work details were not only serious but confidential as well. Having a fellow officer as a partner lightened the load a little.

"Hi, Karen!" Summer shouted as she breezed through the kitchen door. "I thought I heard you." She came across to Karen and gave her a hug and kiss on the cheek.

Karen smiled before glancing across to Zac who looked as surprised and pleased with Summer's unexpected greeting. "Oooh, that's a nice welcome. What did I do to deserve that?"

Summer tilted her head and smiled shyly. "Nothing in particular. The house just comes alive when you're here and Dad always looks happier, and that makes me happy."

Karen felt her heart tug. Summer had blossomed in recent months. Though Karen had worried about her relationship with Zac and how it may have affected Summer, her concerns dwindled as the months rolled by, and Summer opened up. She was a bright, happy child, deftly balancing life between being a teenager and taking the first steps into adulthood. Despite the problems with her mother, Summer had remained level-headed and upbeat.

"Anything I can do, Dad?" Summer asked.

Zac stopped what he was doing and turned around before placing his hands on his hips. He viewed his daughter with suspicion, his eyes narrowing as he studied her. "What have you done with my daughter?"

Summer fixed her dad with a disbelieving look. "Dad, I can't believe you said that. You make it sound as if I'm a sloth that stays in bed all day and doesn't say more than two words."

"Well, usually you're always having hissy fits and storming around the house."

Summer ignored his dig as she pulled plates from the cupboard and set them on the table before grabbing the cutlery.

"While you're making yourself useful, can you get the salsa, guacamole, and sour cream from the fridge?" Zac asked.

"Of course, no problem."

Zac looked across to Karen and whispered, "That is not my daughter."

Karen loved the banter. It made her smile. She had missed this balance in life so much, and though Summer wasn't her own, seeing Summer grow and thrive stirred maternal feelings in her. Karen's eyes widened when she realised what she had been thinking. Her view of life had changed so much since coming to York that it sometimes took her breath away.

Summer came over and stood beside Karen. She picked a few bits of tomato from the bowl and nibbled on them. "Karen, Dad wants to take me on holiday. Will you come with?"

The question made Karen pause whilst chopping up cucumber. She gazed at Zac who looked stunned, before she turned in Summer's direction.

"Your dad and I talked about this. And... it's lovely that you're asking me as well. It is. But I think you and your dad need daddy and daughter time. Don't you think?"

Summer's features changed as a wave of sadness washed over her. She stared down at the chopping board before returning her gaze in Karen's direction. "Please? Dad doesn't get me sometimes. You do. We had a great laugh at the museum, didn't we?"

"Oi, I am here you know," Zac interrupted.

Karen put the knife down on the board and rested her hands on the work surface. "We had a really good time. And I love spending time with you and your dad. It's the highlight of my week. And seeing you always brings a smile to my face. You kind of remind me of me when I was your age. I've got an idea." Karen turned towards Zac, whilst placing her arm around Summer's shoulder. "How about you and your dad go for one week? I'm sure you can put up with your dad for seven days. Just put your Beats on and ignore him."

Zac wagged an accusatory finger in Karen's direction as if to say, "watch it".

"And then the three of us can go away for a week. Somewhere nice. Hot and sunny. Portugal? The Canaries? Majorca? Whatever you like. How does that sound?"

A squeal of excitement tore through the room as Summer clapped her hands and jumped up and down on the spot. "Seriously? Like, proper seriously?"

Karen's eyes widened. "Yeah… like proper seriously!"

"Jesus, now look what you've done. It's like Summer's had a whole tube of blue Smarties." Zac laughed, throwing his tea towel on to the work surface in resignation as Summer raced around the dining table squealing deliriously.

"OMG, Dad! This is going to be epic. This is going to be banging," Summer said, struggling to contain her excitement.

"Right, let's eat, and then the three of us can sit on the sofa afterwards and look online for somewhere we can go. Deal?" Zac suggested.

Summer didn't need asking again as she raced for her seat and sat down in anticipation.

Zac and Karen locked eyes with each other as they exchanged unspoken words, but the smile that broke on both their faces only confirmed that they were just as excited as Summer.

27

THE NEXT MORNING, Karen had a lightness in her step as she strode into the office. The evening before played like a loop in her mind as images reminded her of the fun she'd had with Zac and Summer. Dinner had been great, and she wondered if there was anything in the notion that food always tasted better when shared in the company of others.

After clearing up and loading the dishwasher, the three of them had eagerly settled down in front of the laptop to search for a holiday that they agreed on. Summer had suggested Turkey, recalling a few wonderful experiences friends had shared about the country. With Summer on one side, and Karen on the other, Zac had sat in the middle in charge of the laptop. Karen had proposed Portugal as she had never been there before, but finally the three of them had decided on sunny Majorca and a gorgeous aparthotel in Cala Bona.

Karen smiled as she remembered Summer racing around the lounge in frenzied excitement before grabbing her phone to share the news with her friends. It was a big step for Karen. She'd never been away with a boyfriend, let alone a boyfriend and his daughter. Her holidays had been nothing more than girly trips with best friends where they drank from midday until the early hours before collapsing in bed blind drunk and doing it all again the next day. This "family" holiday felt very grown-up to Karen, and she looked forward to it with trepidation and excitement.

Walking through the doors of the SCU, Karen made her way towards Ed and Preet, whose desks faced each other. Both were busy writing up notes as Karen approached.

"Hey, you two. I just wanted to make sure you were both okay after the post-mortems?"

Ed and Preet looked at each other for a moment before looking up at Karen. Both nodded in unison.

"I'm a lot better today, but I found it hard," Preet admitted. "Ed handled it far better than me."

"I appreciate you both going on my behalf. We hardly ever come across house fire deaths. It's good to get the experience under your belt. If either of you ever want to talk about it, then my door is always open." Karen's gaze darted between both, checking for any signs of uncertainty or concern. When both nodded and thanked her, she asked them to join her at the front of the room for a quick update.

As Karen darted through the desks, she rallied her team. Her phone buzzed in her back pocket. Pulling it out, she tutted when she recognised Henry's number. She ignored the call and stuffed it back into her back pocket.

With her officers gathered around the whiteboard, Karen wished them all good morning. Most of them looked keen and alert. A few faces looked tired and half awake. She appreciated the long hours the team was putting in, as well as the impact it may have been having on their personal lives. Home-cooked meals would go cold and dry in the oven. Kids would go to sleep without a bedtime story, and partners would be asleep by the time her team got home. It was a challenging life for most officers.

"Okay, team. Have we got anything on Dixon?" she began.

Belinda contributed first. "We've looked into his financial background. He is carrying huge loans. By huge, I mean six hundred grand plus. The banks seem more than willing to lend him the money. His three- and five-year projections forecast gross profits of 1.5 million and 3 million, respectively."

A couple of officers whistled as they digested those figures.

One of her junior officers, Claire, chipped in with her feedback next. "We've spoken to a few other farms within the five-mile radius. Dixon approached three of the four farms to express an interest in buying them out."

Karen paced up and down in front of the whiteboard. With her hands stuffed in her pockets, she was deep in thought. The more they looked into Dixon, the more it troubled her. He was a ruthless, unsavoury character.

"What was their opinion of Dixon?" she asked, taking a sip of her coffee.

"They didn't like him. They knew his true intentions right off the bat. He gave them all this flannel about wanting to invest in the area, support the local economy, create new jobs, and give back to the local community," Claire replied.

"And they didn't buy it?"

Claire shook her head. "They didn't have a kind word to say about his mega farm. It's affecting all of their businesses. Their incomes have dropped since he set up. Reading between the lines, they all felt Dixon was trying to put them out of business so he could buy up their farms at a cheaper price."

"He's all heart, isn't he?" Karen replied dryly.

Karen took a few moments to go over the latest information from forensics, confirming the identities of the first three victims, the high alcohol content, and suggesting the booze was the most plausible reason five of the six victims didn't wake as the fire took hold.

Karen's phone started vibrating in her back pocket again. She ignored it whilst listening to further feedback from her team.

"Karen, we've analysed the call logs for William, John and Andrea," Ty began. "I'm still working through them, but there's nothing that jumps out over the last few weeks that raises any concerns for me. A few congratulatory text messages from friends and neighbouring farms. A couple of other messages from suppliers." Ty scanned through a printout in his hand. "There was a call and subsequent voicemail from a mobile number linked to a courier firm. Apparently, John Lawson was expecting a delivery on the afternoon of the fire. Parts for his quad bike, but the driver had broken down on the motorway. The driver showed up at nine thirty p.m."

"Was everything okay?" Karen asked.

Ty nodded. "Yes. John seemed a bit sloshed and was very chatty. The driver, Andreas, dropped off the parts and headed off. He said the family appeared in high spirits. He spotted nothing untoward or suspicious. Andreas pulled up further down the lane and sorted out the rest of his packages, which took him about an hour, before he headed off again."

"Okay. Thanks, Ty. Let's keep working on Dixon. We need something more concrete before I can pull him in."

Karen left the team to it as she headed back to her desk. Her phone rang again in her back pocket. Grabbing it, Henry's number flashed up on her screen. *He's persistent.*

28

KAREN STOOD by her office window and looked out across a small grassy strip of land that skirted around the back of her building. A few trees offered spots of dappled shade. Not a single cloud marred the sky. She sighed dreaming of how perfect that spot would be with a good book and a glass of wine. She dialled Henry's number and waited for it to connect.

"DCI Heath, you're a hard person to track down."

"Henry, just because I gave you my contact details, it doesn't give you the green light to keep calling me," Karen replied sternly.

"Well, I can be impatient at times."

"You think?"

"All right, I get it. Think of me as a little stone in your shoe that keeps annoying you."

"I was thinking more like a boulder," Karen said. "Anyway, what's so urgent?"

"Yes. Right. Okay, the reason I was so keen to contact you was because I thought about our conversation and the Lawsons. It sprung to mind that I wrote an article two years ago that might interest you."

Karen was all ears. "Go on."

"Before I do and considering I'm doing your job for you. What's in it for me?"

Karen sat there dumbfounded by his sheer cheek. "Um, what's in it for you? That you're speaking to the senior investigating officer, and if you're withholding information that might be relevant to my investigation, you could find yourself in a bit of bother."

Henry laughed and cleared his throat. "Hardball. I like it."

Karen's irritation rose and she was about to snap at him down the phone when he continued.

"I covered a car accident two years ago involving Robert Lawson. It was a nasty one. A head-on collision between Robert and a transit van. Robert was speeding on a night out, as do most young locals who know these roads like the back of their hand. His girlfriend was Maria Rutter. She suffered significant facial and chest injuries, and broke both legs. Maria had reclined her seat so at the point of impact it crushed her legs behind the engine bulkhead."

As a PC, Karen had attended multiple RTCs, road traffic collisions, and had witnessed everything from minor bumps and scratches to loss of life, where officers had to search for body parts.

"And what happened to Robert?" Karen asked.

"He escaped with superficial injuries. The blue transit was abandoned at the scene; the occupants escaped across the field. It was a stolen vehicle. Maria came off worse. She was in a coma and on life support for six weeks. Her parents, Colin and Annie Rutter, came close to losing her when her heart stopped. It broke them as they had suffered two miscarriages before having Maria. It was quite a tragic tale because the Rutters thought they could never have children. Strong churchgoers, they believed Maria was a gift from God."

"And what happened after that?"

"Well, in the weeks and months that followed, it blew up between the Lawsons and the Rutters. Colin Rutter blamed Robert Lawson for the accident that almost took his daughter. The police brought no charges because it looked like the stolen van was at fault."

"I see." Karen felt a tinge of excitement at the prospect of a new line of enquiry opening.

"I told you it would be worth your while," Henry boasted.

"Yeah, yeah. What happened to Maria?"

"Depression. Socially phobic. Anxiety. The list goes on. Her parents spent a year caring for her. Maria had to learn to walk again. The family was never the same. Annie suffered a breakdown. Colin struggled to hold things together and their small farm suffered."

"Did you ever meet them?"

"I tried. Believe me I really tried. Colin chased me off his farm twice. Waved a shotgun at me too. Said he'd kill me if I came anywhere near his family again."

"Did you report it to the police?" Karen asked.

Henry fell silent for a few moments.

"Henry?"

"I considered it, but the family had been through so much. I didn't want them getting into trouble any further. It was a warning. I doubt Colin would have gone through with it."

Risky assumption, Karen thought.

"Thanks for letting me know, Henry. I'll look into it."

"That it?" Henry exclaimed.

Karen's eyebrows shot towards the ceiling. "If you're hoping for a medal, you'll be hugely disappointed. Let me look into this first."

"Come on, DC—"

Karen cut the call before Henry finished.

29

KAREN HEADED west out of the city and followed her satnav as it once again took her through rolling countryside and tight, hedge-lined narrow lanes. The address Belinda had given her was a little over five miles away from the Lawson farm. It had popped up on Bel's radar as she'd extended the search to look for witnesses and information.

Having travelled back and forth along these roads in recent days, Karen was getting a feel for the terrain. She knew when to speed up and slow down on certain bends, especially when they were close to gates which led into fields. Her car rumbled over dried mud tyre tracks.

Since Henry's call had led her to being here today, she afforded herself a small smile. He was cheeky but not arrogant. Keen to impress, his persistence had resulted in some benefit for her. As yet, she was unsure what this visit would yield or how, if at all, it was connected to her case. Karen's thoughts were shaken when the satnav announced her arrival at the address.

Karen slowed, looking for the entrance to the farm. Two low stone pillars appeared up ahead on the right. Karen indicated and pulled in. The pillars still had rusty iron fixings attached to them where a farm gate had once stood. Karen scanned the tiny yard pitted with deep grooves and evidence of tyre tracks. The place looked much worse than she had imagined. The farmhouse was smaller than the Lawsons' property. It desperately needed repair as she noticed peeling paint on the wooden frames, patches of brickwork where cement render had fallen off, and a greyish tint to the now faded white-painted walls.

Stepping out and locking the car behind her, out of habit more than anything else, she wondered who would be around to steal it from such a remote location. Karen walked up to the door and, spotting the absence of a door-bell, knocked. It took a few moments before a woman in a thin navy crew neck jumper and light blue jeans answered it. She had short brown hair, parted to one side, thick jowls, and blue eyes cloaked by heavy lids.

Karen held up her warrant card. "I'm Detective Chief Inspector Karen Heath from York police. I'm looking for Colin and Annie Rutter?"

The woman remained expressionless as her eyes travelled from Karen to the warrant card. "I'm Annie Rutter. What's this about?"

"I wonder if you have a few moments. I'm investigating the fire at the Lawson farm and contacting all the farms in the local area."

Annie Rutter's eyes narrowed, her heavy eyelids almost concealing her eyes. She finally nodded and invited Karen in.

Together, they walked through to the rear of the property. Karen glanced at the rooms on either side of the hallway as she passed. The house appeared dated and in need of a lick of paint. The wooden furniture was old and well worn. As Karen followed Annie through to the kitchen, the dated theme continued.

Annie offered Karen a seat at the table before going to the open back door and shouting. "Colin, it's the police."

Karen watched as Annie hovered in the doorway. With one arm folded across her chest, she rested her other elbow on it, and chewed her fingers.

Colin Rutter came in from outside and studied his wife before looking across to Karen. He was a tall man wearing a blue checked shirt and corduroy jeans. With a full head of hair, going grey in places, he walked with a stoop and rounded shoulders.

Annie and Colin Rutter finally joined Karen at the table.

Karen noticed how the pair looked tired and weary. Crow lines spread from their eyes, creases furrowed their brows, and their skin sagged.

"What's this about?" Colin uttered, his voice timid but perceptible. His gaze travelled around the kitchen.

Annie stared at Karen; a vacant expression plastered her face.

There is something not quite right about this couple, Karen decided. They didn't seem with it. It was as if their bodies were here, but their minds were somewhere else. "I'm the senior investigating officer on the case regarding the arson attack on the Lawson farm. I'm sure you know by now that it resulted in the loss of six members of the Lawson family." Karen studied their features. Nothing. No reaction. Not even the slightest flicker of awareness in their eyes. *Strange.*

"I'm wondering if you saw or heard anything on the night of the fire." Karen offered them the date and looked at both. *Nothing. This isn't going well.* Karen couldn't afford to pussyfoot around them any further. "This may be a bit sensitive, but I understand that your daughter Maria was in a relationship with Robert Lawson, the younger son, and they were in a nasty accident."

Karen spotted the first flicker of reaction in Colin's eyes, but he continued with his silence. Annie Rutter locked eyes with Karen for a moment before looking down. Karen sensed a hint of anger.

"I understand you're hurt and angry because Maria was involved in an accident. How was it left between your family and the Lawsons?"

Colin sighed as he stiffened and sat upright. "It's done. What's the point of talking about a family that is dead now? We wanted Maria to have nothing more to do with Robbie. That bloody relationship nearly killed her."

As if on cue, Karen heard what sounded like crutches tapping on the stone floor behind her. She spun to see a young lady lurching along, leaning firmly on her crutches, appearing in the kitchen doorway.

"Maria, this doesn't concern you. Go back through to the lounge and rest," Colin said, his voice low and measured.

Karen turned back to see Colin glare at his daughter before he threw Karen the same stare. The atmosphere became icy as silence fell. Annie Rutter stared wide-eyed at her husband but remained tight-lipped.

"Dad, I'm fine," Maria winced as the tapping sound of her crutches filled the silent void. Maria looked at Karen and smiled through the pain before introducing herself.

Karen stood and pulled out a chair for her to sit, but Maria turned down the offer, choosing instead to look across at her parents.

"You can't keep wrapping me in cotton wool." Maria looked towards Karen. "Sorry about these," she said, nodding towards the crutches. "I'm waiting for a knee replacement. My right knee didn't completely heal after the patella shattered in the accident. I have pins in my right tibia and fibula, and they held together my left femur with screws and a plate. I have more metal in me than most scrapyards." Maria laughed, attempting to inject humour into the situation.

Karen smiled and nodded.

"I heard you talking about Robbie and his family," Maria said, avoiding the scowl on her dad's face. "My mum and dad fell out with the Lawsons after my accident. They blamed Robbie and that led to a few arguments between my parents and his."

"Enough!" Colin hissed, banging his fist down on the table. "This is family business."

"Don't talk to her like that," Annie shouted, jabbing her husband in the arm.

Colin turned towards his wife. "This is family business," he repeated. "No one else."

"Mr Rutter, I think we should all..."

"This is none of your business, either. You need to go," Rutter hissed, as he pointed an accusatory bony finger in Karen's direction.

"I appreciate this is upsetting, but I'm trying to build a better picture of what happened at the Lawson farm," Karen said.

"No. No. You think we had something to do with it," Rutter replied, slapping his hand on the table, making his wife jump.

Annie Rutter pushed back her chair and stared at her husband before storming out, her heavy footsteps thundering up the stairs, followed by the slamming of a door.

"See what you've done," Colin spat as he too pushed back his chair and marched out of the back door.

Karen sat, mouth open, staring at the two empty chairs in front of her. *I wasn't expecting that.*

Maria shuffled around to the side of the table and looked in both directions at the path that both parents had taken. She bowed her head and stared at the floor and sniffed before looking back up at Karen. "I'm sorry about that, but I think you'd better go. You won't get any more answers from my parents now."

Maria looked more tired than she had a few moments ago. Karen wondered if this was a familiar situation in the Rutter household. She studied Maria's face and saw a sadness in her watery eyes. "I'm sorry. Perhaps you could help me with a few questions whilst you're here?" Karen suggested.

"Not today. Please. I don't think it's a good idea. Just go."

"Okay," Karen said, standing. She passed Maria her card. "Here are my details. Perhaps we can talk again in the next day or so. I'll see myself out."

30

"THERE WAS something very odd about that family," Karen said, pulling up a chair alongside Jade's desk and placing her mug of coffee on a bit of paper.

Jade stopped tapping away on her keyboard and leant back in her chair, before swivelling around to face Karen. "How so?"

Karen grimaced. "I get that they're carrying a lot of grief as most parents would in their situation. But Annie Rutter seemed aloof, and Colin, her husband, looked lost in his own thoughts. I studied him for a few minutes and his eyes bounced around the kitchen, first the walls, then the ceiling, then into emptiness. It's like he kept zoning out."

"Mental health?" Belinda interrupted, overhearing the conversation.

Karen shrugged. "Henry Beavis, the intrepid reporter who won't stop bugging me, mentioned that Annie Rutter suffered a breakdown after the accident. Colin fared little better and struggled to hold things together. And to be frank, I think he's still not coping. The farmhouse is in a state of disrepair, the machinery looked like it had seen better days, and… the place looked tatty."

Karen, Belinda, and Jade threw around theories.

"I called Ellen on my way back to see if she'd heard anything." Karen blew the top of her coffee before taking a cautious sip. "She corroborated Henry's feedback. The families had been feuding since the accident with the Rutters blaming Robbie Lawson for injuring their daughter."

Belinda rested her elbows on a desk and interlocked her fingers to form a steeple. "We've spoken to a lot of farming families as we've extended the radius, and no one has mentioned the Rutters. Going on what you've said, and the lack of information we've received, it sounds like they kept themselves to themselves?"

Karen and Jade both nodded in agreement with Belinda's assessment.

"Bel, can you get a few members of the team to dig into the Rutters' background?" Karen asked.

"Sure. Are we looking for anything in particular?"

"Other than the accident involving their daughter and Robert Lawson, check to see if there have been any other incidents involving both families. Arguments. Any complaints. Also, look into their financials."

As Karen continued with her instructions, Belinda tapped away on her keyboard to check the police database. "No formal complaints or incidents on the PNC by either the Lawsons or the Rutters."

"What about the accident involving Robert Lawson? Officers would have been in attendance." Karen said.

Belinda carried out another online search. "Yep. Local and traffic officers attended the incident. They breathalysed Robert Lawson at the scene. He was under the legal limit. The DrugWipe came back negative too. The occupants of the van left the scene and were never located. No charges were brought against Robert Lawson."

Karen thought about her visit to the family. "There was something that Colin Rutter said that sounded odd. When I spoke about the Lawson family dying in the fire, he replied, "it's done." I didn't have time to quiz him on that. My visit was too brief. But it seemed an odd thing to say."

Jade agreed. "It's done as is in the deed is done? Or they're now dead, so what's the point in talking about them?"

"Either, I guess," Karen replied. "Let's see what else we can dig up on them."

Karen was about to continue when Preet joined them.

"Karen, I've been following up on Dixon, as Jade asked me to." Preet smiled in Jade's direction before continuing. "I was looking for any other interactions that Dixon may have had, and this popped up." Preet handed the printout to Karen. "The Environment Agency investigated the potential poisoning of the land on the Lawson farm a year ago. Agency officers conducted a thorough analysis of a stream that cuts through their land. Liquid fertiliser had been discharged into the water. The water was highly acidic, and the fish died."

Karen furrowed her brow. "Liquid fertiliser?"

"Yes, water and soil samples that were taken from the area showed high levels of nitrogen, phosphorus, and potassium. Those are the most common nutrients found in today's commercial fertilisers," Preet continued.

"I assume the agency interviewed John Lawson?" Karen asked.

Preet nodded. "They did. John Lawson was adamant that he wasn't to blame and accused Pat Dixon. Agency officers found no traces of the commercial fertiliser on the Lawson or Dixon properties, but that didn't stop either from owning it before."

Karen scanned through the document. Pat Dixon had been interviewed, fiercely denying the allegations that he'd been responsible for discharging the chemicals into the stream. He'd accused John Lawson of contaminating the water because John Lawson was anxious about competition from other farmers. The more Karen read, the more it painted a bitter and ongoing feud between Lawson and Dixon.

It was the second such incident where the Environment Agency had been called. Someone had alerted them to a slurry spillage in the same area only six months before that. Again, John Lawson denied any responsibility or knowledge for the incident. The investigating team had scrutinised how John Lawson managed his farm, paying attention to how Lawson reduced the risk of slurry run-off or run-through to land drains, and if he'd been in breach of safety protocols by shifting excess slurry to other parts of his farm to disperse it on the land.

Karen looked up from the document, passing it over for Jade to read. "He'd had a rough time of it."

"They examined every detail of how he manages slurry? What the fuck?" Jade remarked, confusion etched on her features. "They examined how he washed his dairy parlours, how he removed the excess using the least amount of water, if he kept his animals on straw during the winter months to produce solid manure rather than slurry, kept uncontaminated surface water away from dirty yards, and kept drains clear in the yard." The list appeared endless as Jade's eyes widened in surprise.

"Exactly. It was as if every aspect of his farming knowledge and business was coming under the microscope." Karen thought for a moment. "*If* this was all instigated by Dixon to drive Lawson out of business, we are dealing with a very dangerous man."

"I'll contact the Environment Agency again and see what else I can find," Preet said before heading back to her desk.

Karen thanked her before rising from her chair and rubbing her eyes with the heels of her hands.

Belinda stepped away from the desk to make a cup of coffee, leaving Karen and Jade to mull over the situation.

"Jade, I think we need to bring Dixon in for questioning. Can you arrange for officers to pick him up? Shall we grab lunch in the meantime?"

"Sounds good to me. I'm starving," Jade replied, grabbing her bag.

31

KAREN PAID for her chicken pasta salad and a can of Coke before lifting her tray from the cashier. She glanced over her shoulder and spotted Jade not far behind. A long queue of hungry officers formed behind her as she dithered over whether to get a jacket potato or a tuna mayo baguette. She couldn't help but smile at the wall of disgruntled faces craning their necks to see what the hold-up was.

"Karen," a voice came from behind her.

Karen turned on her heel to see DI Anita Mani walking past.

"Oh hi, Anita. Haven't seen you in ages. I'm grabbing lunch with Jade; do you want to join us?"

"I'd love to, but I've already eaten. Next time?"

"Definitely. It would be nice to have a bit of a catch-up. I'm really sorry. Things have been utterly chaotic."

Anita waved off Karen's apology. "Don't be daft. I know how it is. Whenever you're free."

Karen noticed Anita looking smart today. A two-piece jacket and trouser combo, black blouse, court shoes. "Meetings?" Karen suggested, looking Anita up and down.

"No. I'm in court this afternoon. A rape trial. I could do with sending my DS. I've got so much paperwork at the moment."

"You look tired. Is everything okay?"

Anita offered a weak smile. "Ash is working crazy shit hours at the moment, and Samara is struggling with uni stuff. I feel bad for not being there for her. I really want to see her."

"Why don't you then?" Karen said.

Anita sighed. "In one word, Ash. He wants to come as well, but he's so mega busy that he can't take the time off."

"Why don't you go down anyway, and plan on going again with Ash as soon as his work frees up?"

Anita shrugged. "I'll try to run that one by him. I'll let you know what he says." She rubbed Karen's arm before scooting off.

Karen grabbed a table, and Jade joined her seconds later.

"There was too much choice. I went for the sausages and chips in the end."

Rolling her eyes, Karen laughed at Jade's indecisiveness.

They spent the next few minutes in silence tucking into their food. Karen kept checking her phone waiting on Dixon's arrival. She didn't envy the officers sent to fetch him. She imagined him kicking off in the back of the car and giving them a hard time.

Karen leant into the table and whispered. "I've got some news for you."

Jade's eyes widened. "Zac's proposed. You're getting married. I need a new hat!"

"Noooo."

Jade peered up towards the ceiling, pondering all the possibilities it could be before she eagerly jabbed a finger in Karen's direction. "You're pregnant! I can pretend to be all grown-up and take your place for a year?"

"Oh Jesus, Jade. No, you don't need a new hat. And no, you can't be acting DCI because you're not a DI yet."

Jade sunk into her seat and pretended to sulk. "Spoilsport," she moaned before continuing with her food.

Karen purposely did the same to annoy Jade.

"Go on. Spill the beans. You can't tell me you've got news and then not share it with me." Jade huffed like a petulant kid.

Karen smiled. She enjoyed winding Jade up, and for a moment, her thoughts went back to Jane, her younger sister, who had died. She'd never shared happy times with her. There was no teasing or bickering, no fights over clothes, no plaiting each other's hair into ponytails, or popcorn and movie nights in front of the TV with their parents. There were no moments of sharing secrets about boyfriends, first kisses, or their first experiences of sex. Jane, having spent most of her time in a residential care home, had never experienced life nor shared a sisterly bond that Karen so hoped for. Jade filled that void, though Jade never knew it.

Karen was jolted from her thoughts when Jade prodded the back of Karen's hand with her fork.

"I'll do that harder if you don't tell me," Jade said, now glaring through narrowed eyes in Karen's direction.

"I'm going on holiday with Zac and Summer. We've booked a holiday to Majorca."

Jade's eyes widened as her mouth fell open. "No way. That's proper grown-up. Fuck. You'll be moving in soon and being a domestic goddess. My God. What did Summer say? Was she okay with that? How does Zac feel about it?"

The flurry of questions tumbled from Jade's lips.

"Summer was the one who suggested it. I wasn't so sure as I thought that Summer and Zac needed time together. But Summer pleaded with me. In the end, we decided that they would go away for a week, and then as soon as they get back, the three of us would head off."

Jade sat back in her chair, speechless.

Karen studied her features looking for a reaction.

"Never did I think I'd witness the day when DCI Karen Heath would settle down. I have a feeling that your wild child days are behind you now." Jade laughed. "In all seriousness, that's fantastic. I think I'm just as excited about you going away as you are. Any chance you could squeeze me into your suitcase?"

Karen's phone chimed. The message confirmed that Dixon was seated in one of the interview rooms.

"Come on," Karen said, pushing her chair back and standing. "Dixon is here. Oh, by the way, no. You can't come.

Taking one kid on holiday is bad enough, but taking two, I don't think my nerves could handle it."

"You cheeky mare," Jade said as she followed Karen out of the canteen.

32

"THIS SHOULD BE INTERESTING. Ready for this?" Karen said as she paused outside the door to the interview room.

"Well, after everything you've said about Dixon, he sounds like such a charming man, I can't wait to meet him," Jade replied dryly.

Karen opened the door and offered up her biggest smile as Dixon and his solicitor looked up from a hushed conversation they were having.

Karen took a seat opposite Dixon, with Jade beside her. Karen did the introductions and the cautions before Dixon's solicitor could get a word in.

Dixon's solicitor was dressed in a grey, three-piece suit, a yellow and black striped tie and a pristinely ironed white shirt. His dark brown hair was gelled and combed back, exposing a large forehead. A tight cut goatee beard framed his mouth.

"I'm Mark Calloway, partner at Calloway and Stevensons solicitors. My client, Pat Dixon, asked me to attend. I'm led to believe this is a formal interview. If so, I would like to hear the exact reasons as to why you've brought him in today." The man stared Karen down as he clipped out each word.

Karen glanced across to Jade for a brief second before returning her attention towards Calloway, offering him another pasted-on smile. "Mr Calloway, no, this isn't a formal interview and your client, Pat Dixon," Karen nodded in Dixon's direction, "is free to go whenever he wants. However, we would greatly appreciate his assistance in our investigation as we piece together any difficulties that the Lawson family may have experienced in the run-up to the fire."

Dixon shook his head and rolled his eyes, before folding his arms across his chest, leaning back and defiantly sticking out his chest.

"Are you suggesting that my client caused difficulties for the Lawson family?" Calloway snapped.

"You can suggest all you want, but I didn't say that. Mr Dixon is part of the local farming community and may have *heard* of difficulties that we are unaware of, so those insights could be valuable to us."

Calloway tapped the end of his gold pen on his pad of paper before throwing Karen the slightest of nods.

These two make a right pair, Karen thought. Calloway was brash, abrasive, and thoroughly unlikeable.

"Mr Dixon," Karen began, briefly glancing at her notes, "as the closest neighbour to the Lawsons, you've already confirmed your approaches to John Lawson about buying his farm on at least two occasions that we know of. Is that correct?"

Dixon nodded.

"Mr Dixon, for the benefit of the tape, could you say your responses please?" Jade asked.

Dixon bristled as he threw a menacing stare in Jade's direction. "Yes," he hissed.

"From what we understand, John Lawson told you in very clear terms that he wasn't interested in selling, but you continued to approach him. Why would you do that?" Karen asked.

Dixon raised a brow. "Everyone has a price. Just because he said no the first time, it didn't mean it was his last answer. *Circumstances* change. A lot could have happened in their lives between my first offer and second. Sometimes all it takes is a poor month, the spread of disease through the herd, the books not balancing, or even a *personal* tragedy, for someone to change their mind." Dixon's voice trailed off as the corner of his mouth curled up.

An uncomfortable silence settled in the room. A deliberate ploy on Karen's part. She was in no hurry to zip through her questions, and the longer she left it, the more frustrated Calloway and Dixon would become.

Calloway sighed and looked at his watch. "DCI, is this interview going anywhere? I do have other business to attend to as I'm sure my client does too."

"I thought you'd be happy to stay here, time is money and all that..." Karen replied, keen to unsettle both men.

"I wondered if you'd be able to shed some light on some information that we uncovered relating to an incident on the Lawson farm. The Environment Agency was alerted about the contamination of a stream that runs through the Lawson farm. It resulted in the surrounding soil being contaminated as well. At one point the stream runs within a hundred metres of your boundary. Did you see or hear anything that may have caused that?" Karen phrased her questions with care.

"No. I'd heard about it obviously because the Environment Agency wanted to check if there was damage to my land. Thankfully there wasn't. Sometimes farmers can be quite reckless with how they manage fertiliser."

Her eyes narrowed as she studied Dixon. "How did you know that I was referring to fertiliser?" Karen probed.

Dixon cleared his throat and glanced across to Calloway, who gave a small nod.

"Because the Environment Agency told me. They also wanted to see if I had any liquid fertiliser, of which I didn't. So, it wasn't me. It's one of those weird mysteries."

"I guess so," Karen replied, not averting her gaze from Dixon's eyes. He had a cocky confidence that Karen despised. "For the record, are you saying that you had nothing to do with the chemical spillage into the stream, nor the slurry contamination that the Environment Agency investigated six months prior to that?"

Dixon stared at Karen for what seemed an eternity, his eyes dark and menacing like a raging storm. "Correct. It sounds like someone was out to get them," he finally said.

"And you wouldn't know who that might be?"

"Nope," Dixon replied with a smile.

Further questioning didn't yield much, but the interview had been enough to let Dixon know that she was on to him. Karen gathered her notes together and nodded in Jade's direction. "Okay, thank you, Mr Dixon, for your time. It's been helpful. We'll be in touch if we need anything else. I'll have an officer show you out."

A few moments later, Karen and Jade stood in the corridor as they watched Calloway and Dixon stride away purposely, a hushed conversation ensuing between them.

Karen's phone pinged in her hand. Glancing at the screen, it was Henry Beavis with a quick one liner.

Any updates?

Karen's reply was just a brief as she shook her head.

No

"The slippery git," Jade muttered under her breath as Dixon and his brief disappeared around a corner.

"Which one?" Karen said, laughing with a huff.

"I didn't like either, but Dixon was so full of shite. He's got more front than Brighton."

"He has, Jade. That's for sure. But that could be his undoing," Karen remarked as they headed back to the office.

33

"So WHERE DO we go from here?" Jade asked as they stood in the kitchen knocking up a brew.

"I'm not sure. Dixon has a motive. He wanted the Lawson farm, and John Lawson had turned him down twice. That makes Lawson a serious fly in the ointment. But he has an alibi, his wife," Karen said as she stirred her coffee, the sound of metal clinking against the inside of her mug.

"That's not the strongest of alibis. If Dixon is a serious contender, then we'll have to pull in his wife as well," Jade said.

"Colin Rutter is a ranked outsider. Mind you, you certainly need to see him first to decide whether he's capable. At times he looked away with the fairies. One minute calm, the next, agitated. But... then again, if he's unstable, his state of mind could have driven him to seek revenge."

The list of suspects was small. CCTV enquiries and a press appeal hadn't turned up anything new. Karen's money was on Dixon.

Karen took a sip of her coffee and then drew in a sharp intake of breath as it scalded her lips. "Shit, why do I do that? Though I think Dixon is in the frame, I can't find any evidence linking him to the scene. We don't have grounds to warrant an arrest. We know conversations took place between him and Lawson. But Dixon hadn't threatened Lawson, nor can we place him at the scene of the fire. There's petrol on every farm, so that's a non-runner. We've got no other forensic evidence linking him to being within a hundred yards of that place, and no witnesses."

Jade grabbed her spoon and Karen's and washed them in the sink before drying them and placing them back in the cutlery drawer. "Dixon must be worried. He came in mob-handed with his solicitor. He either has something to hide or is very shrewd."

Karen nodded as she picked up her mug and strolled along the corridor with Jade beside her. "He has a lot to lose. He's invested a lot of money into his business, expecting huge returns, and has lofty ambitions. Dixon will make sure that everything he does is watertight as he can't afford any mistakes."

"We need to keep digging then, Karen."

Jade was right. The problem was Karen had the shovels but was running out of places to dig. Karen crunched through her ideas for a few moments whilst hovering by the doorway to the SCU. "Okay, two things I need you to do, Jade, put in a request for cell site data for phones belonging to Dixon and Colin Rutter. Let's figure out what their movements were for the twenty-four-hour period leading up to the fire."

"On it."

"Let's get on to the phone companies and see if we can get call logs for both phones as well. We might need to ask Laura to back us up on that one. And also, get someone to look into suppliers or distributors of liquid fertiliser. I want to know who supplies to the farms within a five-mile radius of the Lawsons. I want to know if Dixon purchased any in the past two years."

"Do you think he's going to be that sloppy to put his name on an invoice?" Jade questioned.

Karen shrugged. "Probably not. But one of his minions may have ordered it. Easy enough for him to blame one of his staff for going rogue without his knowledge. Let's see what we can find," Karen said as she moved across the corridor towards her office.

"I'll get back to you as soon as I find out more," Jade replied, disappearing to the main floor.

34

After her interview with Dixon, the afternoon flew by. Karen split the team between working on the Dixon angle and the Rutters, stretching her team to capacity. It had gone six p.m. She'd told her team to go home and get an early night. They had worked tirelessly, as any team would when in the middle of an investigation, but with long hours came frazzled minds and tired bodies. If her team weren't operating at their full potential, Karen worried that mistakes would be made and oversights would happen.

"Don't you think you should go home too?" Jade asked, poking her head around Karen's door.

Karen looked up from her work. "I will soon. More to the point, what are you still doing here? I told everyone to go home an hour ago, and that meant you, too."

"Yeah," Jade replied, "I know. I'm a sucker for punishment. I had a few things I needed to wrap up. Besides, I had the time to spare before I meet James for dinner."

Karen smiled and put on a mock look of surprise. "Looks like things are moving along. From coffee and biscuits to dinner. You're a fast mover."

Jade remained silent for a few moments and offered nothing more than a shrug of her shoulder. "He's good company. It's nothing heavy. We like the same things and get along well. I'm not sure he's my type, but I'm just going with the flow for now, and I think he is, too. It's early days, so your guess is as good as mine what will happen next. We'll have to wait and see."

Jade keeping her innermost thoughts to herself on matters of the heart was something that Karen had noticed a few times since they'd been working together. Karen wasn't sure why. Perhaps it was the fear of commitment. But there was a vulnerability in Jade's behaviour when they spoke. Uncertainty tinged her words. Her shoulders rounded forward as if her arms were desperate to shield her body. Jade furrowed her brow as if her mind were weighing up the risk and benefits.

"I think that's a good shout," Karen said. "You're young. Enjoy yourself. See where it takes you. If it doesn't work out, then that's part of the journey of life. If it works out, then it can only enrich your life and bring you happiness."

Jade's eyes widened. "Shit. When did you become a motivational coach? Move aside Tony Robbins, there's a new coach in town."

Karen laughed. "Go on, bugger off. I'll see you tomorrow."

Jade picked her bags up off the floor and sauntered off down the corridor, leaving Karen in silence once again. There was so much to do, Karen's mind felt as if it was going to explode and split at the seams. She needed progress fast, and Dixon was proving too slippery to pin down as a definite suspect.

"Sod this. I'm going to take my laptop and work from home. I'll sit beside Manky on the sofa with a glass of wine and press lots of buttons on my laptop to look as if I'm busy."

"They say talking to yourself is the first sign of madness," Zac said as he appeared in the doorway.

Karen pushed her chair back and stood up, coming around to the other side of her desk to greet Zac. "It depends on which camp you're in. Apparently, talking to yourself may suggest a higher level of intelligence."

Zac raised a brow as if questioning the validity of her claim. "Perhaps in your little convoluted world."

"I won't argue with scientists at Bangor University. I read an article about it a couple of years ago." Karen stared up towards the ceiling recalling what she'd read. Her eyes widened as her recollection crystallised. She jabbed a finger in Zac's chest. "They said speaking out loud to yourself was found to be a trait of higher cognitive function. So there, suck on that."

Zac moved in closer to Karen and wrapped his arms around her waist. "Well, I popped in to see if you fancied company. But you already appear to have some... Wacko Karen. You two make a lovely pair."

"I'm about to head home. I sent the team home an hour ago, so I deserve an early night too. You're a bit too late."

There was a glint in Zac's eyes as he glanced over his shoulder to check they were alone before leaning in to kiss

Karen passionately, the heat rising between them as Zac pinned her to the wall, his body hungry for her.

"Empty office. No one around. Your desk..." Zac teased.

Karen's heart thundered as she breathed in his aftershave and nuzzled her face into his neck. She wanted him now but slapped him in the chest. "You're terrible and you could get us in trouble. Even though I'm tempted, I'm not going to sprawl out on the desk and risk being interrupted by Carol the cleaner. I'm not sure who would get the bigger fright, us or her."

Zac tried to tempt her, suggesting a quickie instead, but Karen swiftly dampened his amorous thoughts.

Zac followed Karen around to her side of the desk to log off before retrieving her bag and laptop. He rested his hands on her hips and nudged in close behind her.

"Enough!" Karen laughed. "You're terrible. Come on," she said, making her way towards the door, and switching off her office light.

35

MOST OF THE team were in by the time Karen arrived at the office. Weather forecasters had predicted a further rise in temperature over the coming few days, as the country and Karen enjoyed a sustained period of hot sunny days. A marked difference she'd noticed was how the heat was comfortable here compared to London. The air was clean and fresh, and the sun's warmth was hot but not humid. Back in London, long periods of summer heat led to an uncomfortable and choking grey blanket of pollution that hung above the city like a silent assassin. It became difficult to breathe, and the Tubes became unbearable with temperatures topping forty degrees in the tunnels.

"Morning," Karen shouted as she poked her head into the SCU floor. A chorus of replies and a sea of waving hands met her greeting. Her decision to send the team home early had paid off. They looked bright and alert. Karen darted back out and headed for her office. She dropped her bags beside her desk and fired up the computer. Pausing for a moment, she afforded herself a cheeky smile. Her thoughts dashed back to last night and Zac's impromptu visit.

Thinking about it now, Karen felt the heat rise up her neck as she threw a hand over her mouth to stifle a laugh.

"Share the joke."

Karen jumped as the voice startled her. She turned to see Superintendent Laura Kelly leaning against the door frame.

"Ma'am, I didn't know you were there."

Kelly didn't move, a thin smile pressed from her lips.

While Kelly waited, Karen thought fast. "Oh, it was nothing. Zac popped in last night just before I headed home. I was rambling out aloud to myself, running a few ideas through my head." Karen circled with her fingers beside her temples. "He said I must be going mad because I was talking to myself." Karen kept the rest of the conversation, and what happened after that to herself.

"I do that all the time, Karen. I find it useful before a presentation. It helps me to hear whether or not I'm talking absolute bollocks. Most of the time I am."

You're not wrong there, Karen thought.

"Anyway, I wanted to see how we're getting on with the Lawson case."

"Sorry, ma'am. I should have updated you yesterday, but it was a pretty manic day. We've not had much joy on the forensic front. The CCTV trawl hasn't helped either. A lack of CCTV on the farm, and in the lane from both directions, has hampered our efforts. Even the press release yielded little of significance."

Kelly grimaced. "That's disappointing. I suppose you wouldn't have these kinds of problems in London?"

"No, ma'am. Pardon my French, but you can't fart in London without getting caught on CCTV."

That brought a smile to Kelly's face. Karen still hadn't figured the woman out. But from talking with colleagues who'd been here longer, neither had they. The smile from a Trojan Horse was one such comment Karen had heard.

"I've had a new line of enquiry open, ma'am. The Rutters. Another farming family. They've been in an ongoing feud with the Lawsons ever since their daughter Maria was involved in a car accident with her boyfriend, Robert, one of the Lawson boys. She almost lost her life, and the Rutters blame Robert Lawson for her injuries and the ongoing physical difficulties." Karen filled Kelly in on her visit to the Rutters and how strange the family appeared, in particular the parents.

Kelly checked the time on her phone. "Okay, keep me updated. I need to be on a call in five minutes. Come and find me later if you have any more news." With that, Kelly disappeared from the doorway before Karen replied.

"Bye then," Karen said as she made her way into the SCU.

She hovered by Belinda's desk and, not needing a formal team meeting, shouted across the floor to check for any important updates that hadn't been added to the system yet.

"Karen, I put in a request for cell site data for the three members of the Rutter family. None of their phones pinged a tower close enough to suggest that they were near the Lawson farm on the night of the fire," Ed offered.

Belinda chipped in next. "I've contacted households and farms close to the Rutters. The Rutters have very little to do with the locals. They keep themselves to themselves."

"Anything to do with their business?" Karen asked, looking around her team.

A sea of blank faces suggested her team had found nothing. "Can we keep looking, then? From what I've gathered, the business suffered after Maria's accident. Understandably, her parents focused on nursing their daughter, which may have led to their business losing income or even collapsing. That could be a huge driver or motivator for revenge."

A few officers nodded in agreement.

"There's an interesting update from forensics," an officer from her team added.

Dan Kennedy was a short fella with large muscular shoulders, pecs which looked as if they needed supporting with a bra, and thighs as thick as tree trunks. During one of her earlier getting to know you meetings with Dan, she'd discovered he had been an amateur bodybuilder, even coming third place in a national competition.

"Fire away, Dan The Man," Karen prompted.

Dan wiggled his mouse and flicked through his screen. "We didn't find anything of interest on the phones belonging to the dad, mum, and grandad. But the high-tech team did a more extensive recovery of the phone belonging to Robert Lawson. He'd placed his phone in the drawer beside his bed, so even though it was fire damaged, it wasn't as bad as the others."

"Have all the phones been dealt with now?" Karen asked.

Dan shook his head. "Five of the six are done. We should get the results on the sixth phone in the next day or two." Returning to his point, Dan continued, "There was a lot of recent text traffic between Robert Lawson and Maria."

The news piqued Karen's interest. "How recent?"

"As in hours before the fire was reported. The text history goes back months. Messages were exchanged almost daily, sometimes with dozens of messages a day. But that's not the interesting part. It's clear from the messages that Maria Rutter and Robert Lawson were in a relationship, one they kept from their families."

Karen's eyes widened. "You're kidding?"

"Nope. There's plenty of evidence in those text messages to suggest that they were meeting in secret away from both farms where people wouldn't know them. Maria used taxis, telling her parents that she was off for physio treatment. Haxby, Stamford Bridge, Wetherby, even the Travelodge at Tadcaster. Maria would sometimes have someone drop her off halfway, and then Robert would pick her up. It's all there in the text messages."

"No shit. Now that is interesting. Good work, Dan."

"I wonder if Rutter found out about their relationship?" Ty questioned. "It gives us a motive. If the Rutters banned their daughter from seeing Robert, and Rutter found out, it may have been enough to drive the man over the edge, especially after the way you described his behaviour."

"I guess we'll soon find out. I think we need another word with Maria. Good work, team. Jade, you're with me," Karen said.

36

"YOU WEREN'T JOKING when you said this place needed a lick of paint," Jade remarked as Karen pulled into the small yard belonging to the Rutters. Jade leant forward in her seat and peered up towards the farmhouse.

"I think times have been very hard for them. Judging by what we already know about the family, I'm surprised they still have a farm," Karen said, unbuckling her belt and stepping from the car. "Now remember, Colin Rutter has a bit of a short fuse and got agitated yesterday. So he may kick off again." Karen stopped by the front door and knocked before taking a step back and glancing around the yard. Nothing appeared to have changed. The farm vehicles remained where she'd seen them yesterday. A green 4x4 pickup was still parked by the side of the farmhouse. An eerie stillness blanketed the property as if it were suspended in time.

Karen heard footsteps on the flagstone hallway floor before a key turned and the door opened. Annie Rutter appeared and folded her arms whilst blocking the doorway. Her eyes travelled between Karen and Jade, her blank expression giving nothing away to begin with.

"We told you everything yesterday. Please leave us alone. We have nothing more to say," she said in an icy bitter tone.

"I appreciate that, Mrs Rutter. But we're not here to talk to you or your husband. We'd like a quick word with Maria if that's possible. Is she in?"

Annie remained rooted to the spot, her coldness frosting the atmosphere between herself and the officers.

An awkward stand-off ensued for a few moments before Colin Rutter appeared from a side room further down the hallway, his face stern, his eyes cold, his stoop more pronounced as he marched up the hallway to the front door. Karen and Jade took a step back in readiness in case Colin kicked off.

"You have no right coming back here!" Colin barked, jabbing a finger in Karen's direction. "You're uninvited. Get off my land!"

Karen puffed out her chest and remained steadfast. "We don't need an invitation. Mr Rutter, we're investigating the death of six members of the same family. We need to speak to your daughter, Maria. We can do this nice and calm... or not. As I've already said to your wife, we'd like a quick word with Maria."

Colin remained defiant as he stood over the shoulder of his wife. "She doesn't want to talk to you. And you can't talk to her. Not without my permission."

Karen raised her hand, palm facing forward to pacify Colin. "I appreciate what you're saying. But Maria is a grown woman. She doesn't need your permission and neither do we."

Colin's eyes flickered with anger as his jaw stiffened. "You can't enter my property without permission."

Karen was getting sick of his attitude as she glanced across at Jade, rolling her eyes. "Mr Rutter. We are trying to be cordial, but you're impeding a serious investigation. Maria is a person of interest that we'd like to talk to. I'd like to do this peacefully, but if you choose to make things difficult, we'll come back to arrest you for obstruction. Personally, if I were you, I'd stop being argumentative because you are not doing yourself any favours and it's pissing me off. Please move aside and let us have a word with Maria... in private, and then we'll be out of your hair."

Annie looked to her husband before bowing her head and walking back down the hallway. Karen noticed the resignation in Annie's posture, the slouched shoulders, the small steps, and sagging neck. With his objections falling on deaf ears, and sensing defeat, Colin Rutter took a step back and glared at the floor. "She's in the last room on the left," he whispered before disappearing down the corridor as well.

They left Karen and Jade standing in the doorway, looking bemused.

"I'll shut the door, shall I?" Jade remarked to no one in particular as she followed Karen down the hallway.

Karen walked through the open doorway at the end to find Maria sitting on a sofa, a Kindle in her hand, her right leg propped up on a stool. Her crutches remained by her side. There was a sadness that Karen noticed in Maria's eyes, as if she'd been crying.

"Hi, Maria. This is my colleague, Detective Sergeant Jade Whiting. We'd like a quick word if that's okay?" Karen said, moving across the room to stand by the window, whilst Jade stood in the doorway, glancing over her shoulder to check if Maria's parents were lurking close by.

Maria sniffed and wiped her nose with the back of her hand. "I know. I heard it all." Maria glanced down at her top and played with a few loose threads that hung from the hem. "I think I know why you're here," she uttered.

Karen looked across at Jade, who shrugged and nodded to let Karen know the coast was clear.

"I guess it's more difficult for you than your parents realise. Our forensic specialist uncovered a chat history between you and Robert Lawson extending over many months, with your most recent messages being hours before Robert and his family lost their lives in the fire."

Maria sniffed louder as tears broke from the corners of her eyes and snaked down her face before dripping off her chin. Her breath came in gasps as her chest heaved, threatening to release an avalanche of grief that she had kept locked away.

"Maria?" Karen prompted, taking a seat beside Maria and placing a hand on her arm.

Maria looked up, her watery eyes reflecting a tidal wave of sadness. Her chin wobbled as her lips trembled. "We were in love. We wanted a future together."

Karen squeezed her arm. "We know. But I'm guessing that your parents knew nothing about it?"

Maria shook her head as she swallowed air and blew out her cheeks. Spittle flew from her lips. Maria tried to compose herself as she continued. "We kept it secret, meeting away from here."

"Haxby, Stamford Bridge, Wetherby?" Karen said.

Maria's eyes widened in surprise as she looked at Karen and then at Jade.

Karen nodded. "We know."

"It was the only way we could get to see each other. My parents didn't want me going anywhere near him again after the... accident. They blamed Robbie. Dad was so mad that Robbie had nearly killed me. But it wasn't his fault. The police said so. The driver of the van legged it. I was responsible for getting injured." Maria nodded towards her leg. "It was my decision to lie down in the car."

Everything Maria mentioned had already been corroborated at the office. The police report had exonerated Robert Lawson of any liability for the accident and the subsequent injuries.

Karen eyed the young woman with concern. "I have to ask this, Maria. Has your father made threats towards any member of the Lawson family?"

Maria's mouth fell open as she stared at Karen, shock robbing her of her voice as she processed the words. She shook her head. "No. No! Dad didn't do this. There's no way my dad could do anything like this. Dad had an argument with them not long after the accident, blaming Robbie and telling him and the rest of the family to stay away from us. That was it. We've had nothing to do with them since."

"That wasn't quite true. You were in a relationship with Robbie Lawson. Perhaps your dad found out about it?"

Maria shook her head again. "No. I've been too careful. I delete all my messages to Robbie the second I send them. We both agreed to text only at certain times of the day so that even if my phone is left lying around, there won't be a message waiting for me that Dad could find."

Karen asked a few more questions before realising that there wasn't much else she could get from Maria for the time being.

"Okay. Thank you, Maria. You've still got my card. If there's anything else that you can think of, or... would like to talk to me about, call me." Karen squeezed Maria's arm once more before she and Jade left and headed back to the office.

37

"I SWEAR you're going soft in your old age," Jade teased as they parked up and made their way towards their building.

"Shut up. No, I'm not," Karen fired back, opening the door while pushing Jade out of the way to make a point.

"It must be your move that's done something, or you're too loved up. If we confronted Colin Rutter in London, you would have pushed him out of the way, pinned him up against the wall, and growled at him," Jade laughed, following Karen through the corridor.

"Hey, listen. I am more than capable of throwing my weight around when I need to. It's just up here, it requires a different approach."

Jade nodded. "You're right. It does. It requires you to be as soft as a wet paper bag," she said before scooting ahead so Karen couldn't take a swipe at her.

Karen was only halfway down the corridor when she heard heavy footsteps and someone calling her name as an officer chased her. He wheezed as he stopped, then passed on the message that Daniel Lawson was waiting in an interview room for her. Karen thanked the officer and told Jade that she would catch up with her later before turning to head back towards the main reception.

She darted between the buildings, the shade from them providing a welcome relief from the intense sun. The short, brisk walk left her feeling sticky as her blouse clung to her back. Stepping back into the air-conditioned front office, Karen welcomed the cool air as it bathed her face. Interview room three, the officer had indicated. Karen slid the door sign on the front to "ENGAGED" before stepping inside.

Daniel Lawson sat on one side of the table, his fingers locked together. He glanced up with a sullen look in his eyes.

"Daniel, I wasn't expecting you." She wanted to say, "is everything okay?" But of course, it wasn't. The man was grieving for the loss of his brother and the whole family. He would be far from okay. "Is there anything I can help with?"

Daniel's eyes shifted between Karen and his hands. It was as if his words had abandoned him. Karen was in no hurry to rush him and gave him the space he needed before his lips parted.

"I've spoken to Philip, John's solicitor. I'm the only surviving relative on John's side. The farm will be passed to me." Daniel paused for a moment. "Have you found who did this?" Daniel's voice was slow, soft and croaky as if the energy had been sucked from his words.

"Our investigation is still ongoing, Daniel. This is a complicated and challenging case. But I want to reassure you we're doing everything we can to find out what happened on that night and who was responsible. Every one of my officers is focused on this investigation. We want answers as much as you." Karen hoped her words would offer him a degree of reassurance.

Daniel looked up at the ceiling before dragging his hands down his face. "I want answers. My whole family are... gone. Just gone in the blink of an eye." His eyes moistened, forcing him to blink hard. "I keep thinking of the last moments as the house went up in flames. Do... do you think they suffered?"

That was a hard one for Karen to answer truthfully. Five members of the family had died of smoke inhalation where they lay in their beds. She was certain that none of those suffered. But she couldn't say the same for Grandad Lawson, William. Unless he'd fallen and knocked himself out moments after clawing at the windows, she was certain that he had endured a painful death. It wasn't something she wanted to tell Daniel. He was already suffering enough without hearing about the gory details he would hear during the coroner's inquest.

"No. The smoke had overcome them while asleep. They wouldn't have felt anything."

Daniel nodded slowly. "That's good. That's good," he repeated softly. "I blame Dixon."

Karen's brow furrowed, both surprised and curious by that statement. "Why do you say that?"

Daniel sighed. "John had confided in me that Dixon had pressurised him to sell. Twice. John was convinced that

Dixon had contaminated his land to devalue it, so Dixon could buy it at a cheaper price."

"Did John have any proof of that?" Karen asked.

Daniel shook his head and looked in Karen's direction.

Karen noticed Daniel's hands curling into fists. Not a good sign in her book. Non-verbal cues like that always made her wary.

"This is Dixon's fault. He tried to ruin my brother, and I'm certain he was behind the fire." Daniel fell silent for a minute before continuing. "Dixon called me a few hours ago."

Karen sat back in her chair, troubled by this worrying development. "Called you?"

Daniel nodded. He picked up his phone from the table and scrolled through the numbers, finding the most recent call. He turned the phone round in his hand so Karen could see the screen. "That's his number. He called offering to buy the farm." Anger tinged his words as he gripped the phone, his knuckles turning white. "He wants to buy the bloody farm. I've not even buried my family, and that bastard is already after the farm. Something needs to be done about that, or I swear…" he hissed.

The news shocked Karen. She felt anger course through her veins at Dixon's audacity, insensitivity, and greed.

Daniel levelled his eyes at her. "I'm going to find Dixon and…" Daniel thumped his fist on the table.

Karen sucked in a breath. "Daniel. Please don't do anything to jeopardise our case, and don't break the law. Taking matters into your own hands isn't the right way to handle this. You've lost so much already. Please don't lose your freedom by doing something you may regret later."

"I can't sit around waiting for something to happen. You've already told me that this is a challenging case. What happens if you don't find out who did it? What if they get away with it?"

Karen had already thought about that outcome. Not solving the case played on her mind and she didn't even want to consider it. "Daniel, I will not rest until we get a result. I want to find who is responsible too. Please let us do our job," Karen pleaded.

"Well, bloody get Dixon!" Daniel shouted, thumping the table. "Because if you don't, I will." Daniel pushed back his chair and stood up, his hand resting on the table as he leant across. "He... has... to... pay."

Karen held up her hands to pacify Daniel. The man's rapid change in behaviour surprised Karen so much her heart hammered in her chest, but she needed to stay calm and composed. "Daniel, I will speak to Mr Dixon and tell him in no uncertain terms to back off. You have my word on that."

The promise of action appeared to have the desired effect as Daniel paused for a moment and stepped away from the table after gathering his phone, wallet and keys. "Thank you. Sorry for my... my..."

Karen brushed away his concern. "It's fine. Please don't worry. Leave it with me and let me show you out."

"Thank you," Daniel muttered before heading for the door.

38

"EVERYTHING OKAY?" Jade asked as Karen made her way back to her office.

"I've had better days," Karen replied, blowing through her cheeks and running a hand through her hair.

"What's the matter? You look stressed."

Karen groaned as she stopped by her doorway and replied to another text from Henry Beavis who was sniffing for more information. "Daniel Lawson is on the verge of starting World War III. He's pushing for news on our case and places the blame squarely on Dixon's doorstep." Karen took a moment to tell Jade about Dixon's call to Daniel, and how John Lawson had confided in his brother about his concerns that Dixon was attempting to devalue the land.

"You're kidding. What a toerag." Jade gritted her teeth. "He will go to any lengths to get what he wants."

"Yep." Karen's phone vibrated in her back pocket. Pulling it out, she didn't recognise the number straightaway, but answered. "DCI Karen Heath."

A panicked voice screamed down the phone. "DCI Heath, it's Maria. Maria Rutter. My mum and dad are fighting. And I can't stop them."

Karen sensed the desperation in Maria's voice and then heard the argument ensuing in the background.

"What are they fighting about?"

"Everything. I can't... I can't. Please help!"

"Is it a verbal argument? Is it getting physical?" Karen asked, weighing up the severity as she strode into her room to grab her bag, and then curled a finger in Jade's direction asking for her to follow as she hurried through the building towards the car park. All the while, Karen listened in, trying to reassure Maria. Annie screamed first, then her voice became drowned out by Colin shouting back.

"They've both been pushing each other around. Mum's just thrown a plate at Dad. Dad has stormed out of the house."

Karen reassured Maria again that they were on their way, as Jade grabbed one of the pool cars. They raced to the scene, the police sirens forcing vehicles to clear a path for them.

A short while later, Jade silenced the sirens and slammed on the brakes before turning into the driveway of the Rutters' property. Karen flung open her car door and raced towards the ajar front door.

To her right and some distance away from the house, Karen spotted the back end of a red 4x4 she hadn't seen before tucked in behind a trailer. *Looks a battered old Land Rover,* she thought. Karen pushed the front door a few inches, checking to make sure that the coast was clear whilst remaining alert for signs of imminent danger. Taking the first few steps into the hallway, Karen paused, listening for any sound. Jade followed, checking over her shoulder to check no one was coming from behind.

Karen poked her head around each doorway they passed looking for signs of the family. With the eerie silence, a chill crept up Karen's spine at the thought that she might be too late. Visions of several bodies lying in a heap flashed through her mind. With that grim thought haunting her, she heard raised voices again from somewhere towards the back of the property. The further Karen ventured in, the louder the voices became until she reached the kitchen. The shouting escalated through the open back door, coming from somewhere outside.

Bolting past the table and chairs which had been pushed back, Karen and Jade stepped out on to the patio behind the farmhouse to find a red-faced Colin Rutter pointing an accusatory finger at his wife. Tears streamed down Annie's face, her pleas falling on deaf ears, as Colin attempted to push forward. Anger contorted his features, his eyes were dark and heavy like a midwinter storm, his hands had curled into tight fists.

A woman that Karen didn't recognise stood in between the warring couple, her hands placed on Colin's chest, as she attempted to calm the man down. She tried to be heard through Colin's ranting by raising her own voice.

"Calm down! Everything is in hand. You don't need to be like this. It's not helping anyone!" the woman bellowed.

Karen put her in her mid-fifties, with a short, boyish hair-cut, highlighted in places. She had thin lips and a tired-looking face. She was shorter than Colin, but stockier, wearing trainers, jeans, white T-shirt and a thin black gilet.

Maria sat on a chair close by, her head in her hands, her shoulders shaking as she sobbed. Her crutches lay nearby as if tossed to one side.

Karen nodded in Jade's direction, telling her to check on Maria as Karen waded into the melee.

"Enough! Everyone calm down!" Karen shouted as she wrestled with Colin's arm, tugging him backwards to defuse the situation. Unperturbed, the woman continued her efforts to intervene, which only heightened the tension.

Strong words and shouts continued to fly as the jostling continued.

Having had enough, Karen intervened. "I said I would deal with this," Karen said firmly, pulling out her warrant card and shoving it in the woman's face.

The woman recoiled, her eyelids flickering as she bared her gritted teeth.

Karen pushed Colin further into the garden to create a safe space. All the while, he didn't take his eyes off his wife. Karen felt the tension in his stiffened muscles, like a wild predator ready to pounce on its victim again.

"What the bloody hell is going on here?" Karen demanded, jabbing the man in his chest. She glanced over her shoulder to see Jade crouching down with her arm over Maria's shoulder having a word with her. Annie Rutter walked alone around the grounds of the garden, head bowed, whilst the other woman folded her arms and stared at Karen.

Colin placed his hands up in surrender. "I'm fine. Things got out of hand. This is a family disagreement, so I would ask you to mind your own business," he said through laboured breaths. His face was pulled taut, his eyes bulging, the muscles in his neck strained.

"This is my business when your daughter calls me because she is terrified. I want to know what is going on," Karen demanded. "Who's the other lady?"

"My sister, Peggy."

"Your sister?"

"Yes."

"Okay… So, what is she doing here?" Karen asked, looking confused, as she shot Peggy a glance. The bristling woman continued to glare at Karen.

Rutter shrugged. "She just turned up."

"Right, you wait here. Do not move. Do not say a word or I'll arrest you." Karen made her way over to Jade, frequently glancing over her shoulder to make sure that Rutter stayed put.

Maria wheezed. A lattice of red lines filled her eyes as she wiped away the last of her tears. Jade rubbed Maria's shoulder as Karen leant on one knee.

"Are you okay?"

Maria looked at Karen and shook her head. "When will this stop? They just keep arguing all the time. They started pushing each other around, and I didn't know what to do. I can't step in between them to pull them apart when I'm balancing on crutches." Maria's chin wobbled as she stared at her parents. "That's when I called my aunt. And then I called you. I didn't know what else to do. I'm sorry."

Karen rubbed the back of Maria's hand. "Hey, there's nothing to apologise for. You did the right thing."

"She's not bloody going, and that's the end of the matter!" Colin Rutter yelled, causing everyone to look in his direction.

"I said don't... say... a... word!" Karen yelled. "Last warning." She took a deep breath to calm herself. "What's your dad talking about?"

Maria sighed. Her body was loose and limp, a look of hopeless resignation on her face. She looked broken, in Karen's opinion.

"I told my dad I wanted to go to Robbie's funeral when it happens. And that's when he..." Maria's voice trailed off.

Karen looked at Jade, who shared a similar expression to her own. *That wouldn't have gone down well.*

"It's the right thing to do," Maria added. "It doesn't matter that the families don't get on, but I need to be there. I loved Robbie. He would have been there if it was me."

"Maria, I need you to go inside with Jade while I have a word with your parents." Karen watched as Jade retrieved Maria's crutches and handed them over to her. Maria inched back in, glancing once over her shoulder in her father's direction.

"I understand you're Colin's sister?" Karen asked, approaching Peggy.

Peggy nodded, her face giving nothing away.

Karen noticed a hardness in the woman's face. Her expression lacked emotion. There was no warmth, nothing. "Do you live close by?"

"I do. Not far away," Peggy replied, her voice flat and monotone.

"Right, I want you to take Colin back to your place for a couple of hours to defuse things. I think Annie and Colin need the time apart. Annie can stay here with Maria. Don't bring Colin back until he has a clear head. If Maria calls me again, I will make arrests. Clear?"

Peggy nodded with a hard grimace before turning and heading towards Colin without uttering another word.

"Nice to meet you too," Karen muttered under her breath before heading towards Annie. "Annie, I've asked Peggy to take Colin away for a couple of hours to calm things down. I need you to stay here with Maria and make sure she's okay."

Annie looked worried. She chewed on her bottom lip. "But... Colin won't let this rest."

Karen found herself in a hopeless situation, but being called out to domestics was a part of police life. Listening to differing accounts with conflicting viewpoints often made it hard for the police to make sense of the situation. "I've given explicit instructions that should this escalate into another confrontation again, I'll be making arrests."

Annie's eyes widened in surprise.

"Let the situation de-escalate, and perhaps Colin will realise that in the heat of the moment, he likely overreacted. I suggest you and Maria have a cup of tea and some time to calm down and reflect." It was difficult for Karen to say much more than that. Maria had confided in her about the ongoing relationship with Robbie. A fact that wasn't known to Annie or her husband. "I'll call Maria in a few hours to make sure that everything is okay."

Karen and Jade left once Maria felt calm and settled.

39

JADE STOPPED off in town whilst Karen nipped into a café to pick up two iced coffees for them. Karen welcomed the chilled liquid as it settled in her stomach. The heat hadn't peaked for the day yet and standing around in the Rutters' garden had left her hot and bothered.

"That was a bit of a nightmare," Jade said, taking a sip from her drink as she watched the traffic go by.

"Yep. I'm anticipating another call. If Colin Rutter is reacting like this now about Maria's wish to go to the funeral, can you imagine how he'd react if he found out that Maria and Robbie were still in a relationship until he died?"

"I wouldn't want to be in Maria's shoes."

"Me neither," Karen replied, resting her head on the headrest.

"It's going to come out eventually."

"That's what I'm worried about," Karen replied, looking across at Jade and rolling her eyes. "They're an odd family. I get the impression Rutter enjoys throwing his weight around and shouting the odds. As for his sister, Peggy, the way she stood there looking all high and mighty, you can imagine she doesn't take any shit."

"She might be opinionated, but at least she tried to stop the fighting. Peggy did a better job of it than Annie did. Perhaps she knows how to control her brother better?" Jade speculated.

"Well, we'll soon find out in a couple of hours when Rutter returns home. Brace yourself... That's all I'll say," Karen said, placing her coffee cup down and grabbing her phone from her bag. "That reminds me, I need to phone Dixon." Karen retrieved his number and dialled it, placing the call on loudspeaker.

"Dixon," a rough voice replied.

"Mr Dixon, it's DCI Karen Heath."

"DCI. Is this important? I've just had a delivery turn up and I need to deal with that. Make it quick if you can."

Karen raised a brow in Jade's direction who tutted at Dixon's abrasiveness.

"I'm sure you're a busy man. I'm busy too, so I don't want *you* taking up too much of my time either." Karen smiled as she imagined the annoying man's pinched expression. "Daniel Lawson came to see me. I understand you called him regarding selling the farm. He's not happy about that."

"I can't see the problem there myself." Dixon shouted to someone in the background, "No, you fucking idiot, drop the load over there! Have I got to do everything around here? You muppet."

"Charming," Karen mouthed to Jade.

"I think it's insensitive of you, Mr Dixon. He's lost his whole family and not even buried them yet, let alone had the time to grieve. I'm asking you to back off and give him the space he deserves."

"Is that a threat? I don't think your superiors would appreciate that." Dixon laughed.

"Not at all, Mr Dixon. I'm asking you to appreciate that someone is having a tough time at the moment. The business of the farm isn't at the top of Daniel's mind. I'm sure it's a conversation that can be had in the coming weeks and months."

"Time is money. Hashtag business is business. I'm doing him a favour. One less thing for him to worry about."

Karen pressed her lips together as she inhaled through her irritation. "Well, he doesn't see it that way. He feels that you're intimidating him at a time when he is vulnerable. I urge you to back off and give him the space that he needs."

"Intimidating my arse. He's weak like his brother." Dixon paused for a moment. "For the record, I'll give him a couple of weeks and then I'll call him again." Dixon cut off the call.

Karen stared at her phone before looking at Jade. "Can you believe the nerve of the bloke? I'm not liking him one bit."

Jade shook her head in consternation. "He's not got a sensitive or compassionate bone in his body. He's the type of bloke who'll walk over everyone and not look back."

Karen agreed. The more she spoke to him, the more she didn't like him. *There has to be more that we can uncover on Dixon, or is he just too good to make a mistake?*

40

As Jade dropped her off at the Lawson farm, Karen sighed. She felt like she'd spent most of her day in the car driving from one location to another. Jade had another appointment to attend to and promised to pick Karen up in about an hour.

The shuttering to the front door had been unlocked, and a few boxes of personal effects lay stacked to one side of the entrance. Soot-covered framed photographs, a vase, a few lever arch folders with burnt and charred corners, and some items of clothing were all the evidence that remained of the people who'd once lived here. Now their lives were reduced to a few items stuffed in boxes.

Karen hovered in the doorway and looked in on blackened walls, paint peeling off the ceiling, and sticky black puddles on the floors. Footprints littered the floor and marked where emergency service personnel had marched in and out of the property tackling the blaze. Fresh prints confirmed the more recent visitor that Karen was here to see.

"Daniel!" Karen shouted.

It took a few minutes before the sound of footsteps broke the silence, and a figure loomed into view, appearing from the darkness of the burnt-out remains.

Daniel Lawson trudged through the hallway before stepping out into the brilliant sunshine, squinting as the rays from the sun stung his retinas. "Just seeing what I could salvage," he muttered, putting down another box. "There's not much left. Nothing to say that John and his family once lived here," he said with a heavy sigh as he rubbed his hands together and examined his blackened fingers.

There wasn't much that Karen could say. Decades of family history had gone up in flames. The fire had erased lives and stolen memories. "I'm sorry. Thanks for updating the team that you'd be here. I wanted to catch up with you anyway to let you know that I've spoken to Dixon and told him in no uncertain terms to back off." Karen studied Daniel for a few moments. Each time she saw him, he looked more tired. His shoulders were more rounded, his jowls sagged, and there was a hollowness in his eyes as if the devil had sucked the life out of him.

Daniel nodded. "Do you think that will make a difference?"

"I hope so. If he still gives you grief, then I need to know."

Daniel let out another deep sigh as he studied his surroundings. His eyes shifted from one barn to another before returning to the farmhouse over his shoulder. "A few local farmers are meeting here tomorrow to pay their respects. That's good of them."

Karen nodded. She guessed one neighbour wouldn't be here, hopefully.

"Come for a walk with me," Daniel beckoned as he strolled away and headed around the back of the farmhouse and towards the fields beyond.

Though she needed to get back, Karen rushed to catch up with him. She followed Daniel as he walked through the garden, unlocking a gate at the far end and entering a small field. There were no other buildings as far as the eye could see, with fields to the left and right of them. The grass was dry and crispy beneath her feet. The summer heat had dried the ground, making the going firm underfoot. Karen made a point of stepping over the ruts from the tractor criss-crossing the field. The last thing she needed was twisting her ankle on the cragged ground.

"This was his life," Daniel remarked, waving off into the distance. "John's life, our dad's life, and our grandad's. It's been in our family for generations." Daniel's breath laboured as he headed up a steeper incline towards a hedge line at the far end. "The boys should have had this and then their children. Now it's all gone. If I'm honest, I can't stay here. My life is in Wales, and it would be hard to pull my wife away from there. And... I'd be surrounded by John's memories if I remained here. Even if I could rebuild the farmhouse, I'd be walking in his steps everywhere I went."

Sadness tinged her thoughts as Karen walked alongside, remaining silent. Daniel's words reminded her of how much had been lost. Not just the family itself, but the history of past and future generations.

Having followed Daniel through another gate and into a much larger field, Karen spotted an old derelict building in the middle. She followed as Daniel walked towards the ruins, before stopping near a pile of broken rubble and stone.

They both stood in silence, staring at the structure. Karen wondered about its significance and was about to ask when Daniel spoke.

"This is where it all started. This was the original farm-house where my dad was born, and where my grandad, and great-grandad were born too. Bit by bit, the family expanded the size of the farm." Daniel pointed towards the shell. "This is why John would never sell the farm. He didn't want our legacy destroyed."

Karen pursed her lips, understanding the historical significance of the building.

"I've been to see the Rutters," Karen said, changing the subject. "There was a lot of hostility between the families."

Daniel nodded. "Yeah. John was always unhappy about Robbie's relationship with Maria. He put up with it... until the accident. That changed everything. He didn't want Maria having anything to do with Robbie after that. There was even talk of marriage at one point. That's how keen Robbie was on her, but Colin buried that idea. Rutter said he'd kick Maria out if that ever happened."

"Did that affect Maria's relationship with her dad in the end?"

"Yes. They seemed to argue a lot more after that. Colin was always moaning about Maria not listening to him. Then the accident happened. Colin went to pieces. Maria was his little girl. He sat by her bedside day and night. Didn't eat. Didn't sleep. It was touch and go. Think her heart stopped at one point," Daniel said. He stared up towards the sky as if checking his recollection and then shook his head.

"Did Colin and John ever come face to face after that?" Karen folded her arms across her chest as she walked in a small circle and stared at the ground.

"I think so. I can't be certain if it was face to face. But I definitely know that they had words over the phone. Rutter told John to keep his son away from Maria."

"You know much about Peggy?" Karen asked.

He shook his head as the corners of his mouth tugged down. "Not much. I know Maria is very close to her aunt. Robbie had told John frequently. Confided in her more than her own mum, and that pissed off Annie."

When Karen realised Jade would pick her up soon, she turned to head back. Daniel said he would stay, retrieving the last items before locking up.

Jade arrived a few minutes later. As Karen stepped into the car, her thoughts turned towards the Rutters. Could they have played a part in the fire?

41

THE CONVERSATION with Daniel Lawson rattled in Karen's mind as she arrived back at the station. It was clear now that there was a strong animosity between John Lawson and Colin Rutter. But was Colin capable of murder? Karen wasn't so sure. Yes, he appeared to have a temper, but on meeting him for the first time, he looked a broken and dejected man. Distraught at almost losing his daughter? Yes. Strong enough to execute a plan to scare or murder the whole family? Possibly not.

Karen had spent the journey back to the nick updating Jade, who was equally uncertain. And whilst she'd listened to Jade's take on things, Karen's mind had wandered as her thoughts had turned towards Maria. Maria and Robert Lawson were deeply in love, with the prospect of marriage being snuffed out by Colin Rutter. It appeared to have led to cracks appearing in the young woman's relationship with her dad.

After they pushed through the doors of the SCU, Jade headed towards her desk, dropping her bag beside the chair, before planting herself in front of the computer and logging on. Karen moved between desks, getting quick updates from her officers. It was a hive of activity. Some were on the phones while others gazed at their screens as they followed fresh lines of enquiry. She stopped at the incident board. No matter how many times she willed herself not to look at the images, her eyes drifted towards the charred remains of the Lawson family and the SOCO images of twisted and mangled limbs that had contracted in the heat. Her stomach stirred as she felt heat rise up her neck. They were ghastly images, ones that she didn't see that often. Any officer, including Karen, couldn't help but be affected by the grisly sight.

Lost deep in thought, Karen didn't notice Ed come up alongside her. He studied the images in silence for a few moments.

"I feel sorry for Grandad Lawson. He's the only one who experienced a slow and painful death during the fire. It must be a horrible way to go. It bloody hurts when you scald your hand on a hot pan. But to be consumed by a fire that melts and sizzles your skin… and triggers cardiac arrest?"

"Yeah," was all Karen said in reply.

"Oh, Karen. I thought you might be interested in looking at these. Hot off the forensic press, so to speak." Ed passed over a few sheets of paper. "The high-tech unit managed to recover a portion of deleted messages from John Lawson's phone. There were lots of texts between himself and Pat Dixon. A fair few intimidating texts from Dixon offering to buy the farm."

Karen scanned through the messages. A few stood out to her.

Pat Dixon: "There's only so long that you can hold out before you have to give in. I'm offering you a good price."

John Lawson: "I've told you; my farm isn't for sale. Stop hassling me and piss off."

Pat Dixon: "How long do you think it will be before my farms squeeze you out of business? Weeks? Months? Time is ticking. You know it makes sense."

John Lawson: "When are you going to get it through your thick skull? There's not going to be any sale, now or in the future. This farm belongs to my family. Now fuck off."

Pat Dixon: "No need to be nasty. But if you want to make it personal, we can do. But I would watch your step."

"A bit heated," Karen remarked. Her eyes scanned the rest of the document. It appeared to be an ongoing row, with both sides mud-slinging in an attrition of words.

Ed handed Karen another document. "I've split out the details of extracts recovered from a conversation between Colin Rutter and John Lawson. Colin made a threat to kill."

Karen's eyes widened as she took the second document from Ed and scanned the details. The high-tech unit had recovered partial sections of a message. Not being able to view the whole conversation frustrated Karen, but the bits she saw opened a new angle on her investigation.

Colin Rutter: "Keep away from my family. I know your boy is sniffing around Maria."

John Lawson: "Stop blaming my son for the accident. It could have happened to anyone. They're grown adults.

They can do what they want. Maria is a good lass. Thank God she's not like you."

Colin Rutter: "She is. And your boy nearly killed her. He's ruined her life. He crippled her. Keep that shit away from my girl or else."

John Lawson: "Don't threaten me or my family. It doesn't need to end like this!"

Colin Rutter: "I'm warning you and that idiot son of yours. If I see him on my farm or with Maria, I'll shoot him on sight!!!"

Karen turned to Ed and stared open-mouthed. "Shit. Does Rutter have a shotgun licence?"

"Yes. Most farmers do around here."

"That's heavy-duty," Karen added as she read more of the transcript. "Something may have pushed Colin Rutter beyond his threats to harm Robert Lawson," she speculated. "Can you bring him in ASAP?"

Ed nodded and rushed back to his desk, grabbing his jacket off the back of his seat and heading out of the door, taking another officer with him.

Karen turned towards the team and updated them with the most important points from the phone transcripts. "John Lawson was getting hit from both sides. Pat Dixon was desperate to get his hands on the Lawson farm. He was intimidating John Lawson. Lawson was also being threatened by Colin Rutter. I'll hand this out to you in a sec," Karen said, waving the sheets in front of her. "Colin threatened to shoot Robert Lawson if he saw him with Maria. That's enough to bring him in for questioning. Have we got anything else?" Karen said, opening up the floor.

Belinda nodded. "I have. I've been looking into supplies of fertiliser. There is no evidence of Dixon buying any in the past two years. However, along with a few others in the team, we did a deep dive and examined every business that purchased fertiliser from Agro Limited, the main supplier for the area."

Karen's eyes widened. Sensing good news, she crossed her fingers as her pulse quickened.

"We hit a result," Belinda said with a smile. "A tiny subsidiary owned by a company which in turn is owned by Dixon Holdings Limited purchased dry fertiliser on two separate occasions during the past three years. I spoke with forensics. The dry fertiliser has the same chemical composition as that taken from the soil and stream by the Environment Agency. Agro Limited also confirmed that this small subsidiary was the only one that they had supplied to within a five-mile radius of the Lawson farm."

"Bingo! Bloody bingo!" Karen shouted as she fist-pumped the air. "Why on earth didn't the EA pick up on this to begin with? If they'd conducted the investigation properly, they would have found the exact same information." Karen tutted in disbelief. "Bel, can you get on to Agro Limited and find out whose name is on the invoices? And then let's work out if we can tie it back to Dixon. Good work, team. Fantastic work," Karen said, clapping her hands as she headed back to her office.

42

AN HOUR LATER, Karen and Jade sat across the desk from Colin Rutter in interview room three. Ed had brought him in, and Rutter had turned down legal representation. Jade had already done the introductions for the benefit of the tape and provided the caution and the option for him to leave as he wasn't under arrest.

Colin Rutter looked down at the cup of tea in front of him. He cupped it in both hands, examining it as if he were a psychic ready to study the tea leaves at the bottom and tell Karen her fortune. He didn't avert his gaze throughout the caution, his eyes transfixed on the cup.

Karen opened her folder and pulled out the phone transcripts that Ed had given her. She turned round and slid a copy in Rutter's direction.

Rutter averted his gaze before returning his attention to his cup.

"Mr Rutter, I need you to look at this transcript," Karen began, tapping the sheet of paper with her finger.

Rutter didn't respond.

Karen glanced at Jade with a look of exasperation as she pursed her lips.

"Mr Rutter, we've asked you to come in today to answer a few questions. Please take a moment to look at this transcript. This is a partial conversation that we recovered from John Lawson's mobile phone in which you threaten to shoot his son if you ever saw him with Maria again. We take a threat to kill seriously. Have you got anything to say?"

Rutter shrugged. "No."

"How serious were you when you made that threat? If you saw Robert Lawson again, would you have shot him?"

Rutter looked up and looked at Karen. "Perhaps. I made it very clear to Lawson that I didn't want his boy coming anywhere near Maria ever again. *Ever* again."

Karen nodded, taking on board Rutter's reply. She pointed to a particular line. "I want you to read this," she said, giving him a moment before she read it out. "I will not be held responsible for my actions if you or your boy come anywhere near my family again. You'll regret ever crossing my path."

Rutter remained silent, not even acknowledging Karen's statement.

"That sounds like a man on the edge. Someone so desperate to protect his family that he would do whatever it took." Karen leant into the desk, resting her elbows and interlocking her fingers. "Did John or Robert Lawson upset you enough for you to carry out an arson attack on their property?"

Rutter gritted his teeth and stared at the table; his hands curled into fists in front of him. "They wouldn't listen. That boy ruined my daughter's life. I told them to stay away."

"And when they didn't, you set light to their property?"

Rutter shook his head. He looked up for a moment, his face sullen and weary. His eyes were nothing more than dark pools of sadness. He uncurled his fists and tapped his fingers on the table. His lips muttered words in silence as he stared towards the ceiling.

"Mr Rutter?" Karen asked again.

"No. No. Never pay back evil with more evil. Do things in such a way that everyone can see you're honourable," Rutter whispered as he rocked his head back and forth, tears beginning to fill his eyes. "Tears are prayers, too. They travel to God when we can't speak," he added, sniffing. He looked in Karen's direction, a sadness on his face as his bottom lip quivered. "And sometimes life is just hard, and some days are just rough. And sometimes you've just got to cry before you can move forward and act."

Karen's eyes narrowed as she furrowed her brow. She looked in Jade's direction who wore a twin expression of confusion. Colin Rutter wasn't making sense and she wondered if he was fit to be interviewed.

"Mr Rutter, are you okay to continue? Do you need a break?"

Rutter cleared his throat as he looked up and offered a small, weak smile. "I'm fine. What did you say?"

Karen repeated the question.

"No. I didn't set their property alight. I was nowhere near the farmhouse."

"But you had an ongoing feud with the Lawson family. And from this transcript, you were on the verge of carrying out your threats."

Rutter shrugged. "After Maria's accident, my business almost collapsed. Annie and I were at the hospital every day. And while I was there, I couldn't look after the farm. Peggy tried her best, but she struggled to keep it together. All I could think of was that bastard son of theirs. He had put Maria in hospital." Rutter stabbed his finger into the table to make the point.

"How did you cope?" Karen asked.

"Peggy. My sister. My twin sister. She stepped in when she saw how much we were struggling. Peggy kept our farm running."

Karen gave Jade a sideways glance whilst listening to Rutter.

"Peggy stuck up for me. I was going into meltdown. I couldn't tell you what time of the day it was, or even what day of the week it was. Those days merged into one another. And then he turned up."

"Lawson?" Karen asked.

Rutter shook his head. "Dixon. Stepped in like a vulture. He came in and offered us a way out. My debts were piling up, and he offered to clear my debts for a share of the business and the profits going forward. All off the record."

"Right, I see. And did you accept?"

Rutter nodded. "I had no option. It was that or lose the business. Either way, Dixon would have won." Rutter gritted his teeth as his face twisted with anger. "Peggy was furious with Dixon. He has no morals. I had to stoop to Dixon's level, so I didn't lose the business and Robert Lawson was to blame for that. He put my daughter in danger and nearly lost me my farm."

"That's a strong enough motive to seek revenge. Is that what you did in the end? Made the Lawson family pay the price because you sold your soul to Dixon?" Karen asked.

Rutter placed his hands over his face as he cried. "I swear. I didn't kill them."

"Maybe you went there intending to scare them, hoping that they would escape as soon as the fire started. But unbeknown to you, they were so drunk that they couldn't escape and died of smoke inhalation. And that's what's playing on your conscience now. Your plan to scare them backfired with the loss of six lives."

"No. No. I didn't do it. I swear." Rutter dropped his head on the table and wept.

Karen ended the interview not long after, and once he'd composed himself, arranged for a car to take him home.

Did an act to scare the Lawsons backfire? Karen wondered.

43

"HE'S HOLDING BACK," Karen snapped as she slammed down her folder on the desk with more force than she wanted to. She dropped into her chair as Jade took a seat opposite her.

"Do you think?" Jade replied.

"I think so. Yes, he looked a broken man, and I wasn't even sure he was all there, but he was lucid for most of it. It sounded like a bitter feud between his family and the Lawsons. Perhaps threatening to shoot Robert Lawson was something he said in the heat of the moment, and had no intention to do so, but he made that threat."

Jade stared at her nails and picked a bit of dirt from underneath one of them as she mulled it over too. "Maybe so. Perhaps he didn't have the conviction to see his threat through, and rather than confront any of them, chose a less confrontational approach?"

Karen had thought of that as well. Perhaps when push came to shove, he wasn't as brave as he claimed to be. She had seen his angry outbursts, and the heated argument between himself and his wife had been physical with the pushing and shoving, but not violent. It still played on her mind though. Was he capable of killing? Perhaps it was the case that he had intended to scare the Lawsons, and unbeknown to him, they were so drunk that they couldn't escape. Perhaps that was the guilt that Colin Rutter carried.

"Peggy Rutter," Karen said. "She seemed to be the linchpin that kept the family together whilst Maria was in hospital. She stood up to Dixon."

Jade nodded. "She's certainly a force to be reckoned with. I mean, we saw her in action when she was trying to separate the Rutters when we turned up. It might be worth having a chat with her. She might offer an insight into the Rutters that we haven't seen so far."

"Agreed." Karen replied. "I'm still questioning whether Colin Rutter is of sound mind. There were moments in the interview where he didn't appear to be all there. It's a shame we can't access his medical records. We could talk to his doctor, but they would throw patient confidentiality at us. And Colin Rutter isn't under arrest, nor do we have substantial evidence against him."

Karen knew that they would have to get patient consent or determine that in the absence of consent, the disclosure would be in the public interest. Her argument for accessing the records wouldn't be strong enough at the moment for obtaining a court order.

"I think we have to keep digging," Jade said with a shrug.

Karen opened the case file on her computer and scanned for the specific information. She wanted to review the cell site data for Colin Rutter's phone in case she had missed something first time round. She groaned when realising she hadn't. Cell site triangulation didn't put him anywhere near the Lawson farm on the night of the fire. She scanned back through historical data. There was no evidence of Colin Rutter's phone being used in the vicinity for months. Just to appease her own suspicious mind, she checked Annie Rutter's phone and tutted a few minutes later. The same result. Searches against both of their names hadn't thrown up any other mobile phone contracts. She was clutching at straws here, and each straw slowly slipped through her fingers.

Karen pushed back in her chair and drew air in through her teeth. "The Rutters blamed Robbie Lawson for the accident. They also blamed him for their need to take up Dixon's offer when Maria was in hospital and their farm was going to rat shit. And they also blamed him for ruining Maria's future on the farm. It has to be revenge, but we can't place Colin or Annie Rutter near the farm. God this is frustrating." Karen huffed.

"Is there any point in obtaining a search warrant for the Rutter farm?" Jade asked.

Karen weighed up the option and dispelled it for the moment. "Not without anything more concrete. You're going to find a ton of animal crap and petrol on every farm around here. No weapon was used. It's pointless. We need a better handle on Colin and Annie's movements on the night of the fire. We need to rule them in or out." Karen stood and arched her back, the bones in her spine cracking as the tension melted away. "We're working on the Dixon angle. We know he has an alibi for the night, and the team already had a word with his wife who backed up his alibi. If anyone from the Dixon side did this, it wasn't Dixon, but someone employed by him."

Jade stood too. "I'm done for tonight. Fancy grabbing some dinner?"

"And a beer?" Karen asked with a sly grin on her face as she logged off and grabbed her bag.

"Of course!"

44

WITH SO MANY options in the heart of York city centre, Karen and Jade were spoilt for choice. Finally, they settled on a little burger joint called Fancy Hank's Bar and Kitchen, which made Karen laugh, because it was right next door to Coffee Culture where she had met Henry Beavis, the intrepid and overexcitable local reporter.

As they grabbed a table, Karen could see why others in her team had given this spot such high praise. Small, intimate, fun and with portion sizes that widened Karen's eyes in shock.

A cheerful waiter crouched down beside their table. "Good evening, ladies. I'm Dale, and I'll be serving you this evening. What can I get you to drink?"

"Beck's for me," Jade said.

"Um…" Karen froze as her eyes scanned the drinks menu. "I'll have the same."

Dale smiled and furrowed his brow before glancing at both his customers. "Come on. It's happy hour. This is the home of true American French deep south soul food, and the cocktails just bring the food alive." Passion and excitement dripped from his every word.

Karen and Jade exchanged a cheeky glance. Karen couldn't decide whether he was really enthusiastic about this place, or if it was put on to go with the vibe the owners were pitching to their customers.

"We are still on the clock, so we shouldn't," Karen replied.

Jade scrunched up her face. "No, we are not, Karen. We are done for today."

"There you go, Karen," Dale quipped. "A cheeky little cocktail to go with your cheeky little smile?"

Karen blushed before shaking her head at the cheesiness. He was about half her age, but he was charming. "Oh, go on. What do you recommend?"

Dale took his time explaining the different cocktails, before Karen went for the Alabama Slammer, and Jade picked the 'Til The Cows Come Home in honour of Mississippi, because it had crushed Oreo biscuits in it. For food, they chose blackened Cajun chicken and mega mac and cheese to share between them.

Once the cocktails arrived, they sat in silence for a few minutes enjoying them and letting the alcohol do its work. Karen glanced around at the sea of smiling faces, loud conversations, and raucous laughter that filled the air. When two enormous burgers arrived at the next table, her eyes widened into saucers. Enormous was an understatement, and there was no way anyone could hold a burger of that size in their hands and take a bite from it. The young couple who had ordered them sat shocked before breaking out into laughter. The young lady tackled it with a knife and fork, but her boyfriend, keen to impress, grabbed his burger between two hands and attempted to take a bite, only for one of the two beef patties and a slice of tomato to slide out of the back and land with a plop on his plate.

She turned back towards her own food as it arrived, leaving the young man at the next table to hide his embarrassment as he stuffed a few chips in his mouth.

"This is so good," Karen said as she forked another mouthful of creamy warm mac and cheese, whilst Jade nodded, holding a napkin over her mouth as she chomped deliriously on the chicken, her eyes dancing with excitement.

In between mouthfuls, Karen moved on to her favourite topic, Jade's love life. She carried an obsession about what Jade got up to. Part of it was curiosity, but she also wanted Jade to be happy and felt a tinge of maternal responsibility towards her. "You seem to be a lot more relaxed about seeing James these days. Things going well?" Karen said, scraping a bit of blackened chicken off the bone before rolling her eyes at the heat in her mouth.

"Yeah. It's going okay. We're getting to know each other, and I guess, I'm finding out a lot more about him."

"He's looking after you, right?"

Jade's fork suspended in mid-air. "I'm not a kid, Karen."

Karen held up a hand to clarify. "I didn't mean it that way. I meant is he treating you right?"

"Well, if you mean, is he holding the door open for me, and not talking over me all the time, then yes. He has manners."

Karen nodded. "That's all that matters to me. I don't want you to get hurt."

"I know you're looking out for me, and I appreciate it. As you know, I'm not that great at getting into relationships, and always doubtful, so I hold back a bit. Perhaps that's where I've gone wrong. I've never allowed a boyfriend to get too close to me." Jade took a sip of her cocktail and smiled as the warmth tickled her throat. "I guess I've always had a little bit of a protective shield up. But I've got better at trusting my instinct, and if I keep my guard up, then I'm never going to enjoy myself."

"Well, I don't confess to being a relationship expert if my track history is anything to go by, but sometimes letting your guard down reveals a whole new world to you. Look at me. I could never imagine myself settling down with anyone, and most of my relationships happened in a drunken haze where we're talking of days rather than weeks, months or years. And now I've met Zac and Summer, and I can't believe how much it's changed me."

"There's a hat on the horizon," Jade teased.

Karen's eyes widened in shock. "No chance.... Well... Let's see how things go!"

They both erupted into cackles of laughter.

Jade was about to order another round of cocktails as the first round had gone down far too quickly when Karen's phone rang. Karen fished it out of her bag and looked at the screen before rolling her eyes in Jade's direction.

"Karen speaking." Karen listened for a few moments, nodding, before falling silent again. "Right. I see. Okay, I'll be there shortly."

"What's happened?" Jade asked, seriousness returning to her tone.

"We arrested Daniel Lawson and put him in one of our cells. He had a few drinks and confronted Pat Dixon. Words were exchanged, punches were thrown, and it got messy. I need to pop back to the station now."

"You want me to come too?"

"No," Karen said, grabbing the purse from her bag, and sliding three twenty-pound notes across the table in Jade's direction. "Can you settle the bill whilst I dash off?"

"Sure. But before I go, and considering you're paying, I might treat myself to another cocktail," Jade said, throwing a wink.

Karen rose, threw on a jacket, grabbed her bag, and planted a quick kiss on Jade's cheek. "You knock yourself out, love."

45

THE JANGLING of keys and the clanking of the cell door shook the boozy cobwebs from Karen's mind as she refocused.

Daniel looked up and stared at Karen as she stood in the doorway, a forlorn look on his face. His eyes looked heavy. A thin black line for his lips and slumped shoulders did nothing to hide how broken he was.

Karen nodded towards a custody officer to let him know she would be fine on her own. "You okay?" she asked, taking a few steps into the cold and empty cell. A blue plastic-covered mattress. One pillow, and a small blanket were his only creature comforts.

He offered the smallest of nods.

"Why?" Karen asked.

Daniel Lawson shrugged. "He called again. He said now that John was dead, the farm would flourish in his hands and upped his offer by fifty grand."

Karen gritted her teeth. Dixon had ignored her warning. *What a prick.* "So, you went around there to confront him?"

"Well, *your* word with him appeared to have little effect. Whatever you said to him went in one ear and out the other. When he called... That was the final straw," Daniel replied, shaking his head. "I thought I would go around there and have it out with him. Tell him that the farm wasn't up for sale. But he just kept going on... and on... and on. He said I couldn't be in two places at once even though I said I would move back here."

"And would you come back here?"

Daniel sunk back on to the mattress and leant against the cold wall. He shook his head in resignation and stared at his hands as they rested in his lap. "My life is in Wales. Besides, I couldn't come back to the farm. Not after what happened. Yes, I could demolish the farmhouse and build a brand-new one on a different part of the farm. But the memory would still be there. Every time I walked past *that* spot, I'd know it was where John, his family, and my dad died."

"I can't afford for you to get in trouble like this, Daniel. You are grieving and it hurts. But going and seeing Dixon was a bad idea. Not only for you, but for my investigation. Fortunately for you, Dixon doesn't want to press charges, so you're going to be released under caution."

Daniel let out a small laugh. "All part of Dixon's plan. Of course, he doesn't want to press charges. He wants me to feel grateful that he didn't take this any further."

Karen sighed as she leant up against the wall. "Daniel. Please, just leave it. For your own sake and sanity, stay away from Pat Dixon. This is the only time I'll tell you that. I might not be able to help if this happens again. Are we clear on that?" Karen asked.

"How much have you had to drink?"

"Not enough," Daniel replied, grinding his teeth as he curled his hands into fists.

"I'll arrange for an officer to drive you back to your B & B. Stay there. Lay off the booze and under no circumstances speak to Pat Dixon either on the phone or face to face. If he calls you, ignore the call. If he texts you, do not reply. Also, if he leaves a voicemail or a text, delete neither of those. They may be useful in the future. Is that okay with you?"

"Yeah. I hear you loud and clear."

"Right, I'm heading home. I'm tired and I need some sleep. I suggest you do the same as soon as an officer drops you off. You have an important morning. Take care of yourself, Daniel." Karen walked out of the cell and instructed the custody officer to arrange for Daniel to be released before heading home herself.

46

"MORNING, LOVELY PEOPLE!" Karen shouted across the floor as she walked into the SCU unit. In a hand she carried a large tray of croissants she'd picked up on her journey in. "There's breakfast here for any of you that are still hungry?" She placed the box down on the corner of Ed's desk. The second she turned around, a dozen officers converged on her, all eager faces and smiles. "I guess that's most of you then…" she laughed, moving out of the way as the hungry rabble jostled for position, a sea of hands grabbing at the warm treats. It only took a few seconds before an empty box remained.

For whatever reason, Karen felt in a good mood. It was probably due to her having enjoyed a good night's sleep with Manky curled up at the foot of her bed. With no phone ringing during the night, and another glass of wine, she'd drifted off into a deep sleep within minutes of her head hitting the pillow.

Dropping into her chair and firing up the computer, she sifted through a few envelopes that sat on her desk. With nothing of interest or urgency, she tossed them into her wastepaper basket.

She jiggled her mouse and clicked on her inbox, her eyes skimming down the list of unopened emails. One caught her attention. The final forensic and toxicology reports. Though she knew most of their outcomes already, she still hoped that the team had uncovered a new snippet of information. A vital piece of evidence no matter how small, could provide an insight that would give Karen the breakthrough that she needed.

"Yadda yadda yadda," Karen muttered under her breath as she read the details. Smoke inhalation caused the deaths for everyone, excluding William Lawson. They found high levels of alcohol in everyone, excluding William Lawson. They discovered traces of metformin in William Lawson's bloodstream and cross-referenced it with his medical records to confirm he had type 2 diabetes. He also had amlodipine in his blood sample, and again a cross reference confirmed high blood pressure for over ten years.

Karen tapped her fingers on the desk as if playing an imaginary piano. Forensic evidence wouldn't provide the breakthrough needed. She mulled over her options as she stared around the office, as if doing so would conjure up some inspiration. With her fast running out of options, the prospect of updating Kelly later on today sent a shiver of frustration through her. Kelly would be demanding answers, and Karen didn't have any. Kelly was a woman who lacked patience. Long-drawn-out investigations tied up resources, reduced crime clear-up rates, and often led to the Crime Commissioner stepping in to protect their own backside from political backlash more than anything else.

A quick scan through the case file confirmed her fears. They had added nothing new in the last twenty-four hours. They had followed up and exhausted all leads. A lack of witnesses meant an absence of statements on the system. With a heavy sigh, Karen logged off and stood, grabbing her jacket and handbag before heading out. Though this was the right thing to do, she was about to appear in the spotlight of the local press.

47

THE COURTYARD of the Lawson farm hadn't been this busy since the night of the fire. A number of vehicles were parked in two neat lines to the far left-hand side of the courtyard and away from the main farmhouse. Karen parked up behind them and sat in her car for a few moments. Even though a small crowd was gathered, her eyes were drawn to the blackened bones of the farmhouse that protruded through the broken roof.

Leaving her car, Karen made her way towards the structure and hovered a few yards behind the assembled group. They stood in solemn silence, marking this respectful occasion with heads bowed. Since they had their backs to her, Karen couldn't make out any familiar faces, but she craned her neck and saw Daniel Lawson standing at the front, his hands locked in front of him, looking up at what was once their family home.

It took a few more moments before Karen spotted Ellen Turner at the front, with Bonnie by her side. She thought that was a nice touch, but wondered how the dog must be feeling. After all, it was her family home too, and the humans who were once her family were now gone. A heavy feeling hit Karen in the chest when she thought she heard Bonnie whimper at one point. Karen blinked hard to fight the moisture that blurred her vision.

Ellen stood to Daniel's left, with Charles Wagstaff to his right. The trio represented a nice show of support and solidarity. She didn't recognise any of the other faces. A tight knot sat in her stomach at the prospect that Pat Dixon might turn up. But he wouldn't be stupid enough to show his face, would he?

When she heard footsteps over her shoulder, Karen glanced around. Henry Beavis had arrived to pay his respects. They both exchanged a small smile before Henry moved away to watch the crowd from a different angle. A few other reporters also turned up with cameras in hand. Thankfully, they too showed respect by remaining silent.

The gathering continued for about fifteen minutes before the crowd dissolved. Each farmer took a moment to shake Daniel's hand, a few offering a comforting embrace, before they headed back to their vehicles. The touching moment confirmed in Karen's mind how close-knit the traditional farming community was.

"What are your thoughts on this? Have you got a quote for my article?" Henry asked, moving back in Karen's direction.

"Henry. Now is not the time to be asking me for a quote. Besides, we have a press office for that. I've lost count of the number of times I've been quoted out of context."

"DCI, I'm not like that. I came here today to pay my respects. The farming community has lost a good family. I just thought you might…"

Karen raised a hand to silence him. "Then pay your respects, Henry!" Karen replied firmly. "And the answer is no. And stop with the texts asking for updates. I'm sorry. I said I would give you the scoop once the case was closed, but today isn't the day." Karen was about to continue when several other reporters drifted closer to her, attempting to eavesdrop. Karen smiled at them. A few were about to raise their phones in her direction, expecting a comment, but she brushed them off and walked away. Karen blew out her cheeks and decided to take a walk. The stroll around the farm reminded her of what the Lawsons had tried so hard to protect. This wasn't just a farm. This was their identity.

She stopped near the top of one field and turned, taking in the farm from a distance. It was a lovely setting. Cows grunted and mooed in a neighbouring field to her right. But the harder she listened the more she realised that was the only sound. There was no low rumble of traffic from a nearby motorway or a busy dual carriageway. There were no planes scooting from one destination to another. Just blissful silence. With the warmth of the sun on her face, the smell of grass and the stillness, it felt like a little piece of paradise.

Crossing several fields, she stopped at the old ruins of the original farmhouse that Daniel had showed her. A place where his dad and grandad had both grown up. This was a piece of history that Daniel wasn't prepared to let go of, and she understood why. Her lips pursed into a thin line as despair washed over her. She was so desperate to get a result for them. Karen wanted to find the person responsible. But it was this old, ramshackle and decrepit building that pushed her to fight on. She imagined William Lawson running around, chasing chickens as a little boy. It was as if this spot was a little shrine. Daniel had mentioned how John and the rest of his family would often stop by here in quiet reflection and talk about the old times.

Karen wandered around the perimeter of the former Lawson dwelling. It was beaten and broken from every angle. Very little remained intact. The wooden frames resembled windows, the glass broken and long gone. The remnants of a front door hung at an angle from rusty hinges, and the roof had fallen in on itself. But it wasn't that which caught her attention. Her gaze travelled to a spot a few feet from one wall. She stepped towards it, the dry grass cracking beneath her feet. A grave. A simple grave marked by a small slab of marble. The inscription was simple. It read, *Edith Lawson. Beloved wife, mother, grandma. May you rest in peace and your spirit live on forever.* Karen studied the grave. Now she understood why the Lawsons would never sell the farm. It was the family plot. The family's final resting place.

As Karen made her way back, following her original direction, Jade called.

"Hi, Jade. What's up?"

"Are you still up at the Lawsons?"

"I am. I'll be heading back."

"Any chance you could swing by an address? You're the closest officer. The control room had a call from a resident about one mile away regarding damage to a stone wall surrounding her house. It's a small country lane with a few houses dotted along it. The resident is fed up with cars driving at speed down her road. She thinks a car hit her wall a few days ago. Anyway, she saw the notice we had put in the road asking for any information regarding the fire and called."

Karen rolled her eyes. "Really? Is there no other patrol car in the area? Or a rural policing officer?"

"There is, but they're tied up and can't attend until later in the day. It's kind of on your way home. You could pop in and see if it needs a formal police response. I know it's not the thing we need to deal with, but I thought we could do our bit for community policing," Jade laughed.

"Go on then. Ping me the address. I'll be there in a few minutes."

48

HAVING RECEIVED the address of Brayley Lane and dropping it into her satnav, Karen arrived a short while later. The address was a small brick cottage surrounded by a drystone wall. An elderly lady hovered by the front gate, glancing up and down the lane as Karen approached. Pulling up on to the grassy verge in front of the house, Karen stepped out and introduced herself.

"Margot Anderson?"

"Yes, that's me. I wasn't expecting anyone to appear quickly." Margot was dressed in a long, brown check skirt, white short sleeve top and flat sandals. Her silver hair was pulled tight in a ponytail.

"I was in the area. How can we help?"

Margot pulled open the wooden gate and joined Karen on the verge before guiding her towards the far corner of her stone wall. A small section of it had been reduced to a small heap of stones on the floor.

Community policing, my arse, Karen thought with a sigh.

Margot pointed to the damage. "An idiot either hit the corner of my wall or reversed into it. Probably drunk."

"When did this happen?"

Margot scratched her head and stared off into the distance as she trawled through her memory. "Roughly five, nearly six days ago. It happened overnight. I sleep heavily. Not much wakes me," she commented. "I didn't know about it until the postman pointed it out."

"Were you visited by any police officers in the last week?"

Margot eagerly nodded. "I was. The officers asked me about the fire at the farm. I said I couldn't help. I didn't hear or see anything until I ventured out to get my shopping two days later. Barbara in the shop told me about it. Such a shock you know," Margot said, placing a hand to her chest. "Poor family."

Karen bent down and turned over a few of the stones. A few showed traces of red paint on them. Evidence in her mind that the car had hit the wall. Karen stood and glanced up and down the lane. It was isolated. She couldn't see another property in either direction, but one thing she'd noticed on the satnav during her journey was that this quiet country lane ran parallel to the one leading to the Lawson farm. They were a few hundred metres apart. "I can see that you have a CCTV camera mounted on the wall," Karen said, standing and pointing towards the house.

Margot glanced over her shoulder. "Yes, it's aimed towards the drive down the side of my house. Can't be too careful these days, especially because I live on my own."

"Do you mind if I have a look?"

Margot shrugged and invited Karen in. "Mind the mess. I haven't cleaned up yet. With my knees, I take days to clean this place," Margot moaned, shushing the two cats from their cosy spot on the sofa.

"What are their names?" Karen asked, bending down to run her hand along their backs as the cats brushed past her legs.

"The black one is Leo, and the tabby is Pickles," the woman replied as she sat on the sofa and grabbed the controls for her TV.

The cats skulked off towards the hallway, glancing back as if annoyed they had been turfed out from their warm sunny spot beneath the window.

Karen walked over to the window that looked out over the lane. She couldn't see the far left-hand corner of the wall unless she pinned her face up against the glass and looked as far left as she could. It took Margot a few moments to find the footage, which brought Karen's attention back to the woman.

"Ah, here you go," Margot said as she scrolled through the history on the CCTV screen. "It didn't catch much. Just some lights from the car which I reckon may have been responsible. I checked the rest of the CCTV for that night, and no other vehicles passed down this road. It's a very quiet lane. Barely anything comes down here. It's remote, and that's why I haven't moved from here. I like the solitude."

Karen watched as Margot played the tape. The timestamp piqued Karen's interest more than anything else. The date was the same night as the fire at the Lawsons', and it captured a small grainy image of the bottom of a car for a moment in the far corner of the shot until the vehicle pulled away from Margot's property. When Karen checked the time the car left the frame, it was eleven forty-five p.m.

"Did the officers who visited you ask for a copy of the CCTV?" Karen asked.

Margot shook her head. "They asked me about it, but I told them it doesn't capture the road, just the side of my house where I park my car. It was only when I found out about the damage to my wall that I checked the CCTV footage on the off-chance I could see who was responsible." Margot shrugged. "It didn't capture much other than that car." Margot's eyes widened as she raised a finger. "You don't think it's got something to do with the fire, do you?"

"I don't know. But do you mind if I have a copy of this footage?" Karen said, pulling a small USB stick from her handbag.

"Oh, dear. I'm not very good at all that kind of stuff," Margot replied, a worried frown creasing her forehead.

"That's okay," Karen said, stepping forward and kneeling beside the CCTV recorder. "I know how to do it, if that's okay with you?"

"Of course. Of course. Please, do whatever you need to do. I want to find out who damaged my wall."

Karen saved a copy of the footage on her USB stick before thanking Margot and leaving. As she got back in her car, her mind raced.

49

THE MOMENT KAREN arrived back in the office, she dropped off the USB stick with the high-tech unit hoping they could offer an enhancement to the quality of the video footage although she didn't carry much hope. CCTV footage taken at night was often poor quality even if recorded in HD. Also, Karen had noticed how the footage was darker than similar recordings recovered whilst she was working in London. She put that down to a lack of street lighting and the absence of light pollution away from major cities and built-up areas. Since her move to York, Karen had noticed the night sky looked like a black carpet encrusted with glittering jewels.

Before gathering the team together, Karen received a copy of the footage for reference.

"Listen up everyone. We are running out of leads and our lines of enquiry are hitting dead ends. This can happen in complex investigations, which is why they're often long and drawn-out, but we need to keep focused. I've visited

Margot Anderson." Karen turned in Jade's direction. "Thanks for that, Jade!"

"Don't mention it," Jade replied with a smirk.

"Margot is a resident who lives close to the Lawson farm." Karen headed over to the map. A red pin marked the Lawson farm. Other pins identified the Wagstaff farm and Pat Dixon's mega farm. Karen picked up a black pin from the tray beneath the map and leant in before she found Margot's solitary cottage. She pushed the pin in to mark its location.

"Margot suffered damage to her garden wall on the night of the fire. Whether or not it's connected, I'm not sure. I identified remnants of red paint on a few of the stones. I bagged one of them up and drop it in to forensics. Whatever hit Margot's wall left the scene."

Ned looked confused as his brow furrowed. "How does this connect to our case, Karen?"

Karen shrugged. "I'm not sure if it does at the moment. But..." Karen planted her finger beside the black pin. "It's near the Lawson farm. Our team visited Margot in the days following the arson attack. At the time, she was adamant she hadn't seen or heard anything. We were looking for CCTV footage during our first sweep. Margot has a camera to the side of her property but it's not pointing out towards the road... And on first impressions, I would agree. It's aimed at the driveway beside her cottage."

Karen turned towards a large monitor. She pulled up Google Maps on a laptop, the image now displayed on the large screen for everyone to see.

"When I reviewed the footage at Margot's, I noticed the slightest view of the road in front of her house. It appears on the far edge of the screen and is easy to miss if you aren't looking for it. For a brief second, the video captures a small section of the car moving away from Margot's. We believe this car is the one that hit her wall. We also know that Marcus and Natasha were driven off the road by an oncoming vehicle driving away at speed. The two incidents might be connected." Karen ran her finger along the line of the lane outside Margot's. She repeated it with the lane the Lawson farm was on. "As you can see, these two lanes run parallel. Maybe it's a coincidence, but I saw this car time-stamped on camera about the same time as the fire at the Lawson farm happened. Perhaps it could be our arsonist getting away."

Ned looked just as confused as Karen continued her explanation.

"Margot mentioned unless you are *very* local, most people travelling through the area won't be aware of Brayley Lane. But locals will use Brayley to bypass farm vehicles which often choke up or slow down traffic on Hughton Lane where the Lawsons were based." Karen paced around for a few moments tapping a pen on her chin as she thought things through before returning to the map. "What if our arsonist used Brayley Lane to avoid being seen or captured on CCTV, and didn't spot the camera at the side of Margot's house?"

Ned's eyes widened as the penny dropped. "I see," he said with a nod.

"The person driving this car could either be our suspect or witness. Either way, we need to find them. I want all hands on this. Look for any red cars, people loitering close by, or anything suspicious. We only have a small section of the CCTV footage to examine. Most of the footage is of her car and the path that leads around the side of the cottage. None of that will be relevant. It's this little corner of the screen," Karen said, pointing to a still image that she had printed off, "that we need to be concerned with. Every available officer needs to be on this. Split it out by days and divide it amongst yourselves. Get to work on it."

Karen spent the next few hours popping back into the SCU and going around the team looking for updates on their searches. It was going to take time and waiting for results was often the hardest thing for any SIO. She had been involved in cases where a CCTV trawl had taken days and sometimes weeks. They would review hundreds of hours of footage for the slightest shred of evidence that could blow a case wide open. This was something that Karen had experienced frequently. Back in London, you couldn't move without being spotted on a camera which helped immeasurably in gathering clues and evidence. Bars, restaurants, commercial properties, traffic, ANPR and ULEZ cameras (Ultra High Emission Cameras in London used to identify vehicles that do not meet emission standards), all conducted their own video surveillance. If you sneezed, someone, somewhere would know about it.

The saving grace was that they were looking for a vehicle and not looking for a person in a sea of faces.

50

KAREN HAD LEFT the red-eyed crew to continue trawling through the CCTV footage overnight. She had labelled them the red-eyed crew because they were officers who preferred to work nights as a regular shift, or often volunteered for the graveyard shift when resources were thin on the ground during a major investigation.

She dropped her bag and jacket in her office before heading to the main SCU floor. A different vibe greeted her this morning. She sensed an energy in the room that had been lacking in recent days. The night shift had gone home, replaced with a sea of fresh, bright-eyed faces and the smell of a McDonald's breakfast wafting through the air.

"Morning, everyone. Right, who did the McDonald's breakfast run and didn't wait for me to get in?" Karen said, thrusting her hands on her hips and eying up her team with suspicion.

Officers pointed at the guilty party. Ty sunk down low in his seat as if hiding behind his screen would make him invisible.

"Ty! I can't believe you. After everything I've got you?"

Ty raised his head. "Um… what have you got me?" he demanded in his defence.

Karen's brain crawled to a halt. There had to have been something. She kept clicking her fingers as she scrambled to think of anything before her eyes widened as she poked an accusatory finger in Ty's direction. "Croissants!" she shouted. "I laid them on the end of Ed's desk, and I distinctly recall your hand reaching out for one. Guilty as charged. Lock him up and throw away the key," she growled.

Many in the team burst out laughing as they heckled Ty, who closed his eyes and shook his head in defeat.

"You messed with the wrong lady, Ty. For that, you can make me a coffee," Karen added, heading towards the incident board to check for an update. She glanced over her shoulder to see Ty drag his frame from his chair before heading off towards the kitchen. She afforded herself a smirk as he did so. "What do we have so far?" Karen shouted to no one in particular.

Preet chimed in first. "The team did well last night. It looks like they spotted the same car seven times in the last two weeks travelling down Brayley Lane."

Karen turned towards Preet as excitement bubbled inside her. "That's encouraging."

"Here's the interesting thing," Preet continued. "Two of those occasions were during the day. Eleven a.m., and two thirty-seven p.m. However, the other five occasions were all in the dead of night. It was always between eleven p.m. and one a.m."

Karen's lips pursed into a thin line as she nodded. "Can we be certain it's the same car?"

Preet looked in Belinda's direction who continued with the feedback.

"I think so, Karen. The team checked the approximate size and height of the vehicle on those seven occasions compared to the footage you had seen. It appears to match the same size and shape on each occasion. If they're connected to the fire, perhaps they were doing a few reconnaissance or dummy runs?" Belinda speculated.

"Possibly. Perhaps they were trying to work out a strategy to commit the arson. Was anyone able to confirm the make and model of the vehicle?"

Belinda shook her head. "All they could gather was that it had chunky tyres. Possibly more of an off-roader than a car? The footage was in black and white, so they couldn't confirm the colour either. But we're assuming it's darker."

The more Karen thought, the stronger the possibility became that this vehicle or its occupants were connected to the arson attack. Often criminals would scout a location frequently first before committing the offence. One of her officers quickly checked the police database and confirmed that no robberies, burglaries or thefts had been reported in the area in the two weeks before or on the night of the arson attack.

Hearing that, Karen became even more certain that this vehicle was connected.

"Any news from forensics on the stone that I dropped off?" Karen asked, rubbing her temples.

"Nothing yet," Jade said. "They're taking paint scrapings from the stone, but I suggested that someone from the forensic unit visit the scene to look for fragments from the vehicle. Perhaps a broken light lens? A piece of a bumper?"

"That's a great shout, Jade. I saw nothing in particular when I was there, but something might be lurking around in the grassy verge that I missed. Can you let me know if they find anything?" Karen asked.

"Sure."

One of the desk phones rang somewhere towards the back of the room. An officer answered, before making their way towards the front. "Karen, Daniel Lawson is waiting in reception. He wondered if you had a free moment?"

"Did he say what it was about? He hasn't kicked off again, has he?" Karen asked.

The officer pulled a face and shrugged. "Reception called. They didn't sound concerned. I'm just relaying what they told me."

Karen thanked the officer before heading back to her office to grab her notepad.

51

DANIEL GREETED Karen with a soft smile as she walked in. He stood up from his chair and waited for Karen to take a seat opposite him before he sat again.

Manners go a long way in my books, Karen thought, appreciating Daniel's courtesy. She opened her notepad and put her phone on silent.

"This is unexpected. Is there something I can help with? Can I get you a tea, coffee or water?" Karen asked.

"Thank you. I'm okay. I just wanted to let you know that I'm heading back to Wales in the next day or so. There's nothing more for me to do here. I'll be back down again once we've sorted out the funerals. I'd like it if you would attend." Daniel's eyes moistened as he sucked in air through his teeth.

Ordinarily, it wasn't something she would do, but since she felt a closeness to the family, she accepted the invitation. "Will you be attending the coroner's inquest?"

Daniel licked his bottom lip and stared at the ceiling. To Karen it looked as if Daniel was battling with his mind as his eyes danced.

"I'm not sure is my honest answer. I don't think I could listen to the accounts of what happened on the night of the fire or the feedback from the post-mortems. I'd like to remember them the last time I saw them. In happier times. Good memories." Daniel's voice tapered off. "Mmm," he whispered.

"That's understandable. Sometimes it's easier to remember moments from when they were alive. If there's anything I can do to help, you have my number now. I'll update you as the investigation continues."

Daniel fixed his gaze in Karen's direction. He studied her for a long moment. Usually Karen would find it creepy, but she sensed Daniel was hunting for the right words to express himself.

"Thank you," he said. "Thank you for everything you've done so far. You've handled everything with dignity and authority. I'm sorry I messed up with the whole Dixon thing," he said, swirling his fingers in the air. "I think he got to me. A few drinks turned me into a loose cannon."

Karen smiled. "It's fine. No one was hurt. Mr Dixon decided not to press charges. So…"

Daniel finished her sentence for her as he rose from his chair. "So… I'll be on my way. Thank you once again."

Karen stood and offered a parting handshake before seeing Daniel back to reception. They walked in silence to the main door before Karen stopped and turned towards him. "You've been through a very traumatic experience. Losing family in such terrible circumstances will not only fill you with grief, but also questions. Please make sure you give yourself time to deal with your feelings. And, if for any reason things get too much for you, try to get help. The talking therapies and grief counsellors are brilliant for helping you through a difficult period."

Daniel grimaced and stared at Karen for a few moments before nodding and walking back to the visitors' car park.

Karen watched as he drove away. Sadness filled her heart and despair filled her thoughts. She only wished that she'd had better news to give Daniel before he left, but one thing she was determined to do was find the bastard who did this. Karen swiped her card and heard the familiar buzz on the electronic lock as she headed back into the building. As she pulled out her phone to cancel the silent mode, she saw two missed calls and a voicemail message. Dialling into her account, she heard the fraught and tearful message from Maria Rutter. She sounded in a bad way as Karen hit the redial button.

"Maria, it's DCI Karen Heath. Is everything okay?" Karen asked as soon as the call connected.

"I just can't cope any longer," Maria sobbed.

"Do you want me to come over?"

"No. No. Please don't. My dad would freak out."

Karen made her way through the building, nodding silently to officers that she passed whilst listening to Maria. "Something happened at home? Are your mum and dad still fighting?"

Maria sniffed. "No, they are not fighting, just heated discussions. It's like my parents can't stand the sight of each other. The minute one of them talks, it pisses off the other. It's like they have no common ground any more."

Karen walked into her office and took a seat. "Well, I think the tragedy at the Lawson farm has taken everyone by surprise. It's shocked everyone we've spoken to. I know how you must be feeling about Robbie's death."

Just the mention of his name set Maria off as she wailed down the phone. "How am I going to cope?" She cried through heavy gasps of air.

It felt like déjà vu. She'd only been speaking moments ago with Daniel about coping with grief, and now had to repeat herself. Karen suggested to Maria that grief counselling might help, or at least talk to people who weren't connected to the Lawsons or to her own family.

"I know what you're saying, DCI. But I feel so lost and broken without Robbie. Life is going to be so difficult without him. Even though our families didn't know, one day they would have had to have come to terms with it."

Karen remained silent for a few minutes listening to Maria sob down the line. Maria would intermittently stop, blow her nose, before the crying started again.

"Listen, Maria. I'll keep in touch with you and let you know the outcome of our investigation. Hopefully, we can get justice for Robbie and his family. Perhaps then, coping with your grief will be easier to manage. If you need to cry, then cry. Whatever you do, don't hold it in. But please take care of yourself." Karen made sure that Maria was okay before she hung up.

She sighed and leant back in her chair. "At this rate I could set up a website as an agony aunt."

52

KAREN CLOSED her eyes and ran her fingers down her face. Since she was so tired and hungry, every bone in her body ached as she fought the desperate urge to want to close her eyes and sleep. Some days, she bounced with energy, felt mentally alert and fired on all cylinders. And then other days drained her with poor concentration, forgetting things, feeling low, and occasional restless nights where she couldn't get to sleep.

She wondered if she needed supplements to boost her vitality. Long days, little sleep, stress, and a poor diet may have left her body deficient in nutrients. Or were these symptoms early markers for a change in her body. A few friends in their forties had experienced early menopausal symptoms.

Surely that isn't happening to me? Is it? She made a mental note to contact her GP. "Lord, give me more time," she muttered.

"I'm not disturbing something am I?" came a voice from the doorway.

Karen dropped her hands in her lap and opened her eyes to see Bart Lynch, the CSI manager, leaning against the door frame, his arms folded across his chest, a smirk plastered across his face.

Karen laughed. "No. I considered asking for divine intervention in helping me to crack this case, but I think I'll have to rely on good old policing. Social visit?"

"Sadly, not on this occasion," Bart quipped. "I thought I would pop in and give you an update on that stone sample with the red markings on it. We've taken a scraping and sent it away for analysis. I need specialist help with that. I won't bore you with too much detail, but there's an outfit I use who employs specialist infrared spectroscopy to identify molecular structure, chemical components, and a ton of other stuff. But essentially, it's one of the main techniques used for forensic paint analysis."

"Right." Karen nodded. Bart was venturing into nitty-gritty technical knowledge, which often left her feeling confused. "And this will help us do what?" Karen asked, realising she was out of her depth.

"Well, it's important when examining paint to consider the chemical make-up of the paint and the sequence of layering." Bart paused for a moment to check that it was okay to continue. Getting a weak nod from Karen, he carried on with his explanation. "Vehicle paint has three components: the carrier, the binder and the vehicle. These guys will find the different layers. Different car manufacturers have different grades of paint. A midnight blue Ford will have a contrasting chemical composition to a midnight blue Vauxhall or BMW. I'm hoping the paint analysis will help us identify what manufacturer and perhaps even what model of car had that unique paint composition."

"I see. So, the paint is like a unique identifying tag which will tie it back to a certain make and model?" Karen asked.

"Correct," Bart replied with an affirmative nod. "That's why it's often so hard for garages to match up the right paint with the right vehicle. In order to do so, they need the make, model, and year of manufacture to narrow down what paint sample they need. To the naked eye, two midnight blues would look identical. But under analysis, they would be different in terms of different chemical composition and viscosity. And that ends this Open University lecture on automotive paint analysis. Tune in for the next exciting episode!" Bart winked and chuckled to himself.

"Okay. Thanks, Professor Lynch. Don't forget your white lab coat next time," Karen teased as Bart darted out of the door.

53

KAREN'S SMILE lasted long after Bart left her office. He had his nerdy moments but was also so laid-back that at times she wondered how he did his job. She glanced at the time on her PC and knocked off early. Thinking there wasn't much food in the house, she could swing by the supermarket and do the weekly shop. Then she'd head home and tidy up before enjoying her long hot shower, a bit of a pamper, and then a pizza and movie in front of the TV with Manky curled up beside her.

Karen logged off, and as she did, realised she couldn't remember the last time she'd chilled on her own for a whole evening. She usually spent her free evenings and weekends with Zac and often Summer too. Back in London, the life of a singleton was often a lonely and drunken one from experience. Perhaps that was why people knew her as a workaholic. She would rather do anything than sit at home reflecting on life and the feelings of loneliness. Maybe that said something more about her than anything else. After all, London offered a rich and vibrant nightlife. There was just as much to do during the day. Museums, walks around the Royal Parks, the café culture that lined the uber-trendy streets in Clapham, Notting Hill, and Peckham, and amazing foodie hotspots like Borough Market and Seven Dials Market.

So why had I struggled so much with loneliness? It was a question that Karen had avoided many times in the past for fear of what she would have to admit to herself. In part, it was because she'd spent much of her childhood alone. With her sister being unwell, Karen had been left to play in the garden alone or draw in scrapbooks because her parents had been too busy juggling a household and caring for their sick daughter. Her past had led her to go full steam in the opposite direction, doing whatever she could to keep herself busy as she'd moved through adulthood, seeking solace at the bottom of a wine glass, and filling her life with many flings and one-night stands to feel loved and wanted.

Karen smiled as an image of Zac popped into her thoughts. Being with him changed her entire perspective on life. Their blossoming relationship changed *her* as a person. She didn't ache for affection, and loneliness was a thing of the past. Zac was always there for her. Something else had changed too... she was comfortable being on her own. Karen breathed deeply, closed her eyes, and exhaled slowly. There was so much she was grateful for now.

Switching off the lights in the office, Karen closed the door and headed down the corridor.

"Karen," Ed's voice came from behind her.

Karen let out a small sigh before turning. "Yes, Ed."

"Got good news for you. A few of us have been looking into red vehicles. I know it's early days and we're still awaiting analysis on the paint scrapings, but we thought we'd dig deeper. Anyway," Ed checked his notepad, "we may have a potential lead. We've been looking at owners of red vehicles within a rough five-mile radius of the Lawson farm. So far, there are seven vehicles."

"Okay. And anything of interest?"

Ed nodded. "We've checked DVLA records and eliminated them one by one. Here's the interesting thing. Pat Dixon... owns a red 4x4. It's a 2013 Mitsubishi L200 long wheel-base Barbarian. It might be worth checking out?"

"Good old Pat Dixon. He is never far from our radar. Can you send me the reg, and I'll stop in there on my way home?"

"Sure. Will do, Karen."

Karen was about to turn and leave when Ed stopped her again.

"We've also got another brilliant result regarding our enquiries with the fertiliser company, Agro Limited." Ed's voice bubbled with excitement; his face animated as his eyes lit up. "It took a bit of digging around but Teilo Limited, who purchased the fertiliser, is owned by Clayton Limited which is owned by Dixon Holdings Limited." Ed checked his notes. He speculated that Clayton Limited was registered overseas, possibly for tax benefits or diversification. "Anyway, Darren King, whose name appears on the invoice from Agro Limited, ordered and signed for the fertiliser. Employment records show that Darren King receives his health benefits and pension from Dixon Holdings Limited. They centrally handle all employment records and salaries for every single member of staff across all subsidiary companies under the Dixon Holdings Limited umbrella."

"So regardless of whether or not Pat Dixon knew about it, we can hold him liable for negligence even if he denies all knowledge…" Karen nodded. "Brilliant work, Ed. Send all that information to the investigating team at the Environment Agency. It's their investigation. They can bring the prosecution."

As she fished her car keys out of her bag, Karen looked forward to seeing Pat Dixon squirm in the coming weeks.

54

ON ARRIVAL at Dixon's mega farm, Karen parked a short distance away from the reception block and rather than head there first, decided to snoop around unaccompanied. A few vehicles were parked outside the reception block, and several others nearest to the first few poultry sheds, but she couldn't see any red vehicles matching the description on her phone.

Karen continued to peer around units and down narrow access routes before ending up in front of a large open field where the first signs of construction had begun using large diggers and piledrivers. She glanced over her shoulder in awe of the operation. Everything was on a gigantic scale but as with her recent visits, there appeared to be a distinct lack of staff. She recalled Dixon mention how automated his operation was, right down to the timed mechanical delivery of food for the hens. This worked in Karen's favour because she could wander around without being stopped.

Turning to retrace her steps, Karen headed back between
the nearest two large steel structures, which were more than
the height of a two-storey building. The overpowering
smell assaulted her nostrils. She scrunched up her face and
placed a hand over her nose as her eyes watered. It smelt
like ammonia as it somehow wormed its way into her air
passages and irritated her lungs. She didn't see anything of
particular interest. No red vehicle in any direction. Every
time she came to the crossroads between four units, she'd
glance in each direction. Wheelbarrows, wooden pallets
stacked with feed, hosepipes and shovels, but no red
vehicle.

From somewhere in the distance, she heard the familiar
bellowing voice of Pat Dixon booming instructions into his
walkie-talkie. His commands were broken up with static
while he waited for replies. Expletives filled the air as his
anger grew with whoever he was speaking to. Karen
wanted to dart back in the direction she had come from but
knew Dixon would spot her.

It took a few moments before she turned a corner and saw
Dixon, red in the face, sweat on his brow and sweat patches
on the armpits of his blue shirt. He paused in mid-sentence
when he spotted Karen. His face gave nothing away as he
stared at her.

Karen had to think fast. "Ah, Mr Dixon. I've been looking
for you. I wasn't too sure where you were, so I thought I'd
have a wander around to see if I could track you down. But
I heard your voice before I saw you."

Dixon frowned before clipping his walkie-talkie back on to
his belt. He marched towards Karen, closing the distance
between them. He folded his arms across his chest, his

enormous belly pushing his shirt out and over his belt. "Reception didn't tell me you were here?"

Karen clicked her fingers and rolled her eyes. "Oh, shit. Sorry. I forgot to pop in there and ask for you. I just parked up and headed off. My mistake." Sarcasm dripped from every word.

Dixon's cold and fiery glare speared Karen in place. His eyes were black with hate. "You need to be careful walking around places like this. There's a lot of industrial equipment and machinery. I *wouldn't* want you getting hurt. Haven't you heard about the number of industrial *accidents* that happen on farms? These are dangerous… places."

Karen put on a cheesy smile as her eyes widened. "I'm glad you put safety so high on your list of priorities. That's very reassuring."

"DCI, I'm a very busy man. Is there a reason you came to see me? A phone call would have been far quicker."

"I understand that you have a red 2013 Mitsubishi L200 Barbarian?" Karen asked.

Dixon looked confused as he narrowed his eyes, viewing her with suspicion. "And?"

"Could I take a quick look at it? A witness reported seeing a red vehicle in the area on the night of the fire and it may have sustained some damage. After checking with DVLA, I found there's a red vehicle registered to you."

Dixon laughed and shook his head as he marched off. He wagged his finger in the air. "DCI, you're clutching at straws. But I'm happy to show you it. This way," he barked without taking a moment to see if Karen followed.

They zigzagged through a few units before making their way towards a different part of the farm that Karen hadn't been to yet. Up ahead, a few old stone barns remained, the remnants of the old farm that once stood on this land. They were evidently not in use. The roofs were in disrepair, the rendering between some stones had failed and fallen away, and wooden windows were missing their glass panes. Karen followed Dixon towards the rear of one barn where several vehicles stood in a line. One of them was the red Mitsubishi.

Dixon stopped beside it and waved Karen on to examine it at her leisure. "There you go. Knock your socks off."

Karen approached the vehicle and walked around looking for signs of damage. Scratches littered the bodywork. Dents in the doors, rear quarter panel, and tailgate suggested it had seen better days. Karen ran her hand along the bodywork, picking up dirt on her index finger as she went on.

"It's not been used in a long time. It's covered in dust," Dixon said, a small smile adding to his smugness.

Karen stepped away from the vehicle and examined it from a distance. It had similar chunky tyres to what she had seen in the footage, and the red paint appeared to be a similar shade to what she had discovered on the stone. The space between the wheel and the wheel arch looked of similar size to the one in the video footage, but she couldn't be certain that it was the same vehicle.

"Just because it's covered in dust doesn't mean it hasn't been used. It's been hot and sunny for weeks now. The ground is dry and dusty. It could have been driven across a field or dusty track only this morning and picked up all this dust," Karen replied, before stepping back towards the vehicle and heading around to the other side away from Dixon's view. There was damage to the bodywork above the rear bumper. She spotted a small strip of red paint clinging to the bodywork. Snapping it off, she curled it into her palm before standing. "Have you got any objections to the police forensic unit examining this vehicle? It would be helpful for us to rule it out of our investigation."

Dixon laughed again. "DCI, knock yourself out. You can't prove anything. I've got more important things to do, so you can see yourself out. You know the way back to the main entrance. I expect you to be gone in the next ten minutes," Dixon barked as he glared at her one more time before storming off.

Karen made her way back to her car before getting a small paper evidence bag from her boot and dropping the paint sample into it. She would drop this off with forensics first thing in the morning and arrange for them to make a visit here. A gut feeling told her that this wasn't the vehicle, but then again, she wouldn't put anything past Dixon to cover his tracks.

55

FEELING REFRESHED and a bit more human in the morning, Karen entered the station complex and headed for her office moments after stopping by forensics. The previous evening had been shorter than expected because of her visit to Dixon's farm, but she'd welcomed the chance to knock off early and have the time to herself.

Remaining upbeat was her mantra for today as she strode with purpose, smiling and saying hi to officers who passed by. She bumped into DI Anita Mani who was hurrying to a meeting.

Anita grabbed Karen by the arm, a sense of urgency stressed her features. "Hi, Karen. Listen, I can't stop now. Have a meeting in five minutes. Are you around for lunch next week? Or we can grab a bite after work? Either works for me."

"That sounds great. How about after work? That way, we're not stressing about getting back to our desks. We can chill and have a few drinks and have a really good catch-up?"

Anita smiled. "That sounds like heaven. A night off from listening to Ash's moaning!" she said, rolling her eyes. "Let me text you later," she shouted as she dashed off.

Karen smiled. *As brief encounters go, that was up there.*

"Stay upbeat. We can do this. We need to crack this case," Karen muttered to herself as she pushed open the door to her office and came around to her side of the desk, dropping her bag to one side as she switched on her computer. With little traction yesterday, and the team getting restless, there was a real risk of this investigation stalling. It wasn't the situation Karen wanted. Without evidence and witnesses, she feared the case would be scaled down and resources deployed elsewhere.

Karen opened the case file on the police database and scrolled through the latest updates. There was nothing further on Rutter or Dixon. An email from Karen's boss dampened her mood slightly. Detective Superintendent Laura Kelly was chasing for an update. She groaned at the prospect of seeing Laura later on this morning.

She spent the next half an hour going through and responding to relevant emails before deciding that she needed a break. Locking the screen, she left her office and headed for Zac's. She found him poring over paperwork, head propped up by his hands, and oblivious to Karen's arrival.

"There's me thinking I had the delicate footsteps of a herd of elephants."

Her arrival startled Zac as he sat back in his chair wide-eyed. "Shit, I didn't hear you come in."

"Well, that's obvious." Karen dropped into the chair opposite him. "You didn't even reply to my good morning text!" she growled.

Zac closed his eyes. "Sorry. I saw it as I was driving in. I had a bit of a rough night last night. Summer wasn't well. I was back and forth with a hot water bottle and paracetamol."

"Aw, bless. She okay?"

Zac nodded. "I think so. Stomach cramps."

"She started her periods yet?" Karen asked.

"Not yet. I guess it's not far away because she's had a few of these stomach crampy things in recent months. She's also exhausted and walks around with arms folded across her chest looking as if she's in a bit of discomfort. I've always asked if she's okay, and she just nods and says she's fine. I'm not even sure when they start. But I want to make sure she's okay with it. I'm just not sure if she'll confide in me. How many daughters confide in their dads about periods?"

"She might not be far away. They often start around twelve or thirteen. It sounds like she's experiencing some symptoms leading up to her first period." Karen paused a moment and decided whether to say anything but went ahead anyway. "Listen, I know I'm not her mum. And she needs her mum as she goes through this stage of her life. But... if she doesn't want to talk to her mum, she could always talk to me?" Karen suggested with a shrug.

"That wouldn't bother you?" Zac asked.

Karen smiled. "Of course not. I love Summer. I can have a word the next time I see her. Maybe it might comfort and reassure her to know that she could open up to me about things like this and then not feel so awkward around you. But please say if I'm overstepping the mark," Karen added, raising her hand in the air.

"Do you know you're bloody amazing? If we weren't in the office now, I'd be all over you like a nasty rash."

Karen threw him a sly grin. "Well, that didn't stop you the other night!"

Zac's face reddened in response.

Karen was about to continue when Zac's phone rang. Picking it up, he listened and then paused the caller. "Yes, she's here. I'll pass the message on. Thanks."

Karen looked perplexed as her brow furrowed.

"That was Jade. You're needed back at the SCU. There's been a development."

Karen jumped from her seat. "How did they know I was here? I didn't tell anyone."

Zac smirked. "This place has eyes and ears everywhere. Jade knows you too well."

Karen promised she would call him later before dashing back to her team.

56

KAREN PUSHED through the doors of the SCU unit harder than she wanted to, sending the door flying back and almost into the face of one of her team, Pete, who was heading out. The officer jumped back, a look of surprise and shock on his face.

"Whoa!" he said staggering backwards, the file tucked under his arm almost slipping from his grip.

Karen gasped and threw a hand over her mouth. "Oh my God, Pete. I'm so sorry. Are you okay? I nearly took your face off."

Pete grinned. "I'm fine. That was a close call. I almost got a free nose job!" he laughed as he scooted around Karen and disappeared into the corridor.

Karen shook her head at her clumsiness as she made a beeline for Jade's desk.

"Jade, what's the development?" Karen asked, pushing Jade's paperwork to one side and planting one butt cheek in the space created.

"Whilst you went to see lover boy, the rest of the team have been working *really hard*," Jade teased.

"Oi, you cheeky cow. I was only gone five minutes."

"Yeah. Yeah. You part-timer. Anyway, the paint analysis request from the stone you recovered was fast-tracked. The results just came back. It's a unique tone used by Land Rover on the Freelander, the Discovery, and more recently the Evoque. They dated this paint sample to be at least fifteen years old."

"That rules out the Evoque. That came out around twenty fifteen?" Karen speculated.

"Twenty twelve," Jade replied, correcting her.

"That rules out Dixon's Mitsubishi as well. Bollocks."

"It does. The paint analysis revealed an eighty-three per cent probability that this composition of paint was more likely to be found on the Freelander than the Discovery, simply because more Freelanders were made with that tone of red paint than the Discovery."

Karen's mind went into warp overdrive like the Starship Enterprise as images and memories tumbled through her mind. It took a few moments for the cogs to align until it hit her.

"Shit. Peggy Rutter. She has a red 4x4, not sure what make or model though. It was there when we turned up and it was kicking off. She was off our radar for most of the investigation because she was outside the five-mile radius. Pull her address off the system. We need to pay her a long overdue visit, and arrange for another unit to meet us there," Karen said, hurrying back to her desk to grab her bag.

Thirty minutes later, Karen pulled up at the address for Peggy Rutter. A small Ford Astra patrol car was positioned on the lane beside the house. Throughout the journey, Karen and Jade had thrown theories between themselves, and the more they discussed it, the stronger Peggy's motive had become.

Peggy's address was at the edge of a tiny hamlet, a small dead-end road with three houses. As Karen and Jade got out, Karen scoped the area. Quiet. Just the sound of bird chirps, whistles, and knocking coming from surrounding trees. The slightest hint of a warm breeze stroked Karen's face as she headed towards the property. It appeared modest from the outside, two small windows on either side of the front door, three further windows on the first floor. Karen noticed the overgrown front garden. Tall blades of grass and wild flowers brushed past her ankles as she walked up to the door.

"PC Jarvis and PC Taylor. Where do you want us, guv?" one of the two officers asked as he locked his car and joined Karen.

A ripple of excitement coursed through Karen's body as she pushed through the rickety gate and approached the front door. Karen knocked and glanced towards Jade. When there was no answer, she knocked again.

Turning to her uniformed officers, she asked one to remain out front, whilst the other came with them. "Let's check around the back," Karen said, guiding the way as she stepped through what felt like a mini-orchard. As she turned the corner, she stopped. Parked at the far end of the property was a red Freelander, and on first sight, the vehicle appeared to have the same rear as the one she'd seen at the Rutters'.

"This looks interesting," Jade said as she neared the vehicle and crouched down, pointing towards the rear offside quarter panel damage. "There's a bit of white dusty residue. Perhaps a bit of sand and cement from the stone wall?"

Karen frowned as she leant in to take a closer look. "Possibly. The damage appears to be around about the height of the wall." Karen took out her phone and took a few pictures before pulling up a still image she had taken from the CCTV footage. Stepping back to get a better perspective, Karen held her phone up alongside the vehicle to gain a comparison. "Hmm. It looks the same or similar. The space between the top of the wheel and the wheel arch matches. It's got the chunky wheels as well."

"Let's try around the back?" Jade said, walking past the vehicle and turning left.

The small back garden was as unkempt as the front. A small washing line was strung up between two trees, a few white blouses, a couple of pairs of jeans, and a grey skirt hung from it, drying in the warm morning sunshine.

Karen tapped on the back door. It was old and wooden, with green paint flaking off it from years of neglect. The window frames either side had fared little better. A constant cycle of rain and sun through the seasons had taken its toll. Karen stepped towards the window and peered in through the glass. A dated kitchen loomed into view.

Jade tried the door and looked at Karen in surprise when she realised it was unlocked. Pushing it open, she stepped back in readiness in case anyone came charging out.

"Hello. It's the police!" Karen shouted. When no response came, she shouted louder. "Peggy Rutter, are you there!?"

They waited a few moments in case Peggy was somewhere else in the house. It soon became clear that the house was empty. Karen nodded in Jade's direction before she led the way. Though the kitchen was dated, it was clean. A few soup bowls were stacked up on the kitchen worktop, cereal packets were lined up in size order, and a silver kettle that had seen better days rested on a wooden chopping board. Karen touched the surface of the kettle. Cold.

There were two further rooms. One a lounge, the other a dining room. Both were clean and functional. If Peggy Rutter had been here recently, she had cleared up to make the place presentable. Magazines were stacked up on the coffee table. Fresh flowers sat in small ornate vases on the windowsill, and framed photos of the family hung in one alcove. Karen noticed that even though there were a few pictures of Colin and Annie, pictures of Maria, her niece outnumbered them.

"Peggy!" Karen shouted from the bottom of the stairs.

"Maybe she's dead in her bed and thousands of maggots are eating her body," Jade remarked, raising a brow.

Karen narrowed her eyes in Jade's direction and studied her sergeant. "Really? How the hell does your mind work? I worry about you sometimes. And, if she was decomposing, we would have smelt it by now," Karen said, shaking her head as she took the first few steps.

The upstairs was no different from the rest of the property. And yet there was still no sign of Peggy. It appeared as if Peggy lived alone, the bedroom wardrobe only containing women's clothing.

Making their way downstairs and back out through the rear of the property, Karen let out a deep sigh as she scanned the landscape. It was a few moments before something caught her eye. She nudged Jade and nodded towards the direction of her gaze.

57

KAREN PUSHED through the small wooden gate at the back of the garden and headed into the adjoining field. On any other visit, Karen would have enjoyed the time wandering around the tall grass and listening to the breeze rustling their tips. But her attention was drawn a hundred yards to the far left-hand side of the field where a small summer house stood nestled beneath a large mature tree with graceful branches and bark carved by Mother Nature herself.

Noticing movement through the windows, Karen, Jade and PC Taylor separated, keeping some distance between them as they approached. Karen paused as the door opened.

Peggy Rutter appeared, a dirty scowl on her face as she glared at her visitors in a way that suggested they had trespassed on her land. With her arms behind her back, she took a few more steps to close the distance between herself and the officers before brandishing a shotgun from behind her.

Karen gasped and froze, exchanging nervous glances with Jade and Taylor. Taylor looked terrified, and Jade fared little better as her face twisted into a pained grimace.

Karen held out a hand whilst nodding in Taylor's direction, implying that he should back away. "Call for armed back-up," she whispered to him.

Taylor didn't need another prompt as he stepped back slowly, his eyes trained on Peggy, ready to hit the ground if she raised the barrels without warning.

"Jade, you can step back too. We don't want to crowd her."

"Fuck that, Karen. I'm not leaving you alone. This could go south any second," Jade uttered.

Karen's heart thundered in her chest as a flashback flooded her thoughts. The event played back in her mind of when a convoy that she had organised to take a key witness to court had come under an armed attack, resulting in the death of two officers who were gunned down in cold blood. The witness had been kidnapped, bound, and executed before being dumped. The subsequent fallout had led to her suspension and demotion.

It was as if history was repeating itself again. She couldn't afford to put herself or Jade in the firing line. Karen took a few steps back and held out her hands to pacify the woman. "We're here to talk to you, Peggy. There's no need for this. Why don't you put the shotgun down so that we can talk?"

A tense stand-off followed for what felt like an eternity.

"I wondered when you'd be paying me a visit. I didn't intend it to be like this. I only wanted to frighten them," Peggy declared as she cradled the shotgun in her arms as if holding a baby.

Karen nodded. "I know. But doing this isn't helping. How about you put it down, and then we can talk?"

Peggy shook her head defiantly. "There's no point. No one listened then, and no one is listening now. The Lawsons nearly destroyed our family. And now we are indebted to Dixon."

"I hear what you're saying. But we are listening. I'm listening right now. Just you and me. Why don't you come with me to the station, and you can give me your side of the story? There's already been too much tragedy. Let's not add to it."

The distant wail of sirens punctured the air. Karen knew she was moments away from the situation being taken out of her hands as AFOs, the advance firearms officers, would take control of the situation. The last thing she wanted was more blood being spilled.

"Peggy, we really have little time. I want this situation to end peacefully for all of us. I have more police officers on the way, and they will not take too favourably to you waving a shotgun."

Peggy snarled and took a step forward. "Why does that matter to you? It's not you who nearly lost your brother. It's not you who nearly lost your family business and a way of life."

The noise became louder as sirens quickly approached the property. Mere minutes remained for Karen to de-escalate the situation so no one got hurt.

"I understand loss, Peggy. I lost my sister not long ago, and I know how much it hurts. But doing this will not help anyone. Things are changing for your family. You have to believe me," Karen pleaded.

"They're not!" Peggy screamed, lifting the barrel of her gun and pointing it in the air in defiance.

Karen's breath caught in her throat as her chances of defusing the situation slipped through her fingers. Her thoughts were being drowned out by the sirens and the screech of tyres. Minutes turned into seconds. Karen glanced over her shoulder. Her eyes widened. The first few AFOs streamed through the back garden and into the field, their sights trained on Peggy. Shouts tore through the air, expletives echoed around her.

Karen raised her hand towards the advancing officers, hoping to slow them down.

"Don't move!" one yelled as he moved forward with speed, staring down the barrel of his Heckler & Kock assault rifle, whilst his partner advanced with her Glock handgun trained on Peggy.

Further tactical officers piled through the garden and made their way towards the scene.

"Stand down!" a firearms officer shouted. "Stand fucking down!"

"Hold your position. DCI Karen Heath," Karen demanded. "Give me a minute."

The officers came to a halt just yards from Karen, their sights still trained on Peggy.

Peggy held her ground, not an ounce of fear in her eyes as she glared at the officers.

"Peggy, I really don't want this to end badly. Please, listen to me. Things *are* changing in your family. You have to believe me. The stuff with Dixon is over. He won't be bothering you any more."

Peggy averted her gaze from the officers and studied Karen for a moment.

Karen nodded. "It's true. And... Maria needs you." Karen noticed a change in Peggy's eyes. They flickered. Her lips parted. Karen nodded again. "She will need her auntie more than anything else in the coming months and years. She trusts you. She loves you. She needs you. Please... put the gun down before it's too late."

The realisation hit Peggy as her eyes widened. She cleared her throat and blinked hard as if coming out of a mind trance that had taken over her being. She kneeled and placed the shotgun on the floor before standing and taking a few steps back.

The AFOs hurried forward and secured the shotgun whilst cuffing Peggy.

"Peggy Rutter, I'm arresting you on suspicion of arson and the murder of six members of the Lawson family," Karen said with a sigh as she watched Jade come alongside Peggy and take her by the arm.

58

AN HOUR LATER, Peggy Rutter was sitting in an interview room opposite Karen and Jade. Jade had provided the caution and set up the recorder. Peggy had refused the offer of legal advice as she bowed her head and fiddled with her fingers in her lap.

Karen started with a few questions to get the ball rolling and make Peggy feel comfortable before she moved on to the more pressing issues.

"Peggy, were you responsible for the arson attack on the Lawson farm?"

Peggy looked up for a moment and then nodded.

"Peggy, I need you to verbalise your answers for the benefit of the recorder," Karen stated.

"Yes," was Peggy's solitary reply.

"Why?"

Peggy glanced around the room for a few moments, not eager to reply or to move the interview along. "Because of what they did to my family. They destroyed my brother. After the accident, my brother lost more and more of his identity to where he wouldn't even get out of bed, let alone shave or work the farm. Colin and Annie were suffering. Maria may have been suffering emotionally and physically, but my brother and his wife were suffering too. They weren't strong enough to deal with this. It tore them apart."

"So you blame the Lawsons?"

"I do. Robbie in particular. Maria is like my daughter. The daughter I never had. We are this close," Peggy said, crossing her fingers. "Robbie took away Maria's livelihood, her freedom, and her life. They had to pay, especially because my brother nearly lost his business, and because Dixon bailed us out. That shitbag now has a stake in our family business. And it's all down to Robbie Lawson. Without him and his reckless driving, none of this would have happened. My brother would own *all* of his business, and they would all still be alive."

"That wasn't your decision to make," Karen said.

Peggy leant into the table, her eyes moist, grief stretching her features. "You don't get it, do you? Colin and I are twins. I'm older than him by about three minutes. We think the same. We feel the same. Sometimes I sense his stress, and when I call, I can hear it in his voice. And I feel the pain here," Peggy spewed, jabbing her chest with her index finger. "I... feel... his... pain."

"Did you and your brother Colin plan this together?"

Peggy shook her head. "No. He doesn't know it's me who did this. I can't stand by and see him suffering. They came so close to losing Maria. Did you know Annie had suffered two miscarriages before Maria?"

Karen remained silent, hoping Peggy would fill the void.

Peggy took a sip of water. "After the second miscarriage, they were convinced they could never have children. God had chosen them to be the unlucky ones. And then... Annie fell pregnant. It was as if they'd been given another chance. Then the accident happened, and they watched on helplessly as Maria clung on to life. It was the straw that broke the camel's back when Maria's heart stopped in hospital." Peggy's stare was hard and cold as she glared at Karen. "I'll never forget the look on my brother's face. I didn't feel sadness, only hate. I hated Robbie Lawson for what he had done to my Maria."

Karen checked her notes and took a sip of her water before continuing. "So why take it out on all of them?"

"They weren't supposed to die. I just wanted to scare them."

"You did more than that," Karen said. "The whole family had been celebrating being awarded a new contract with a chain of supermarkets. There was a high level of alcohol amongst five of the six victims. They died of smoke inhalation because they were too drunk. William Lawson, the grandfather, was the only one who was sober enough to try to escape, but as you are aware, he's wheelchair bound most of the time. He died a slow... and painful death."

Peggy looked away, her bottom lip trembling. "I didn't know. I thought the fire would wake them and they'd have time to escape."

"How did you get into the property? Did you know that the side door was unlocked?"

"I did. Robbie had told Maria. It's not uncommon. Lots of farmers around here keep their doors unlocked. As you know, the back door to my cottage was unlocked. I saw you."

"Why didn't the dog bark when you entered?"

Peggy's face softened as a small smile formed on her lips. "I met Bonnie a few times when Maria and Robbie were dating before the accident. She's a good girl. Maria had left one of Robbie's jackets at my house, so I wore that. Bonnie must have recognised his scent. I let her out and ushered her away before I spread petrol over the bottom of the stairs and through the hallway to the back door. I soaked the doormat in petrol before setting it alight."

"Tell me why you parked your Freelander so far away?" Karen asked.

Peggy's chest rose as she took a deep breath before her shoulders sunk. "I didn't want to be noticed too close to the scene. I parked some distance away and made my way across the fields so that I wouldn't be spotted, but when I hurried back, I put the car in reverse instead of drive and crashed into a wall before driving away."

Karen stopped the interview not long after and headed back to the team to debrief them. A current of excitement rippled around the team as they listened.

"Really well done to all of you. You've worked so hard and that's resulted in a confession. Peggy's attempt to scare the Lawsons took a turn for the worst and ended in tragedy.

Let's get the file across to CPS and push for a charging decision ASAP. I'll update the super."

59

KAREN and her team had waited anxiously all afternoon for a decision from CPS, but when the news had come through, the result had been worth it. However, it didn't make Karen's visit any easier as she knocked on the door of the Rutters and waited for someone to answer.

Annie's weary face appeared through the crack as she pulled the door open.

"Hello, Annie. Do you mind if I come in? We've had a development in the case."

Annie's eyes widened as her lips pursed into a thin line before she stepped away from the door and led Karen into the lounge. Colin Rutter cast a desolate figure as he sat slumped on his sofa. Maria sat opposite him, her leg up on a stool, crutches beside her on the floor. Annie went and sat beside her husband, her eyes searching Karen for clues as to her visit.

Karen looked around at the three members of the family. The news was about to deal another hammer blow to an already beleaguered family.

"There isn't an easy way to say this, but earlier on today we arrested Peggy Rutter. Following her interview, she's been formally charged with the arson attack and murder of the Lawson family."

There was a notable gasp from the Rutters as they exchanged glances between them and looks of sheer horror.

"No. No. She's not capable of doing anything like this. You have it wrong," Colin protested, his face red with rage.

"I'm sorry, but she's admitted it as an act of revenge for the Lawsons destroying your livelihood, and for Robbie Lawson almost taking Maria's life. It's clear she has a very strong loyalty to you, Colin."

Colin stared ahead, shock leaching the colour from his face. Tears rolled down Annie's cheeks as she placed an arm over her husband's shoulder in consolation.

Maria sobbed into her hands. Hot tears streamed down her face, and she squeezed her eyelids shut in the hope her tears would stop. "No," she wailed. "Can I see her?" Maria's question came through choppy breaths.

"I'm afraid not at the moment. I'm really sorry. I'll see myself out." Karen rose and made her way from the lounge into the hallway and towards the front door. The clunky sound of crutches soon caught up with her as Karen stepped out into the yard.

"DCI!" Maria shouted through ragged breaths as she tried to catch up.

Karen stopped by her car and turned around to see Maria hobbling towards her, her eyes puffy and red, salty wet trails snaking down her cheeks.

"There must be a mistake. This can't be right," Maria argued, searching Karen's eyes for an answer.

"I'm sorry, Maria. She's confessed. We're sure that Peggy is responsible. We've recovered certain items from her house which lend weight to her being at the scene of the crime."

"I... I don't know what I'm going to do. Peggy was like my big sister. I told her everything and now I've lost Robbie and Aunt Peggy. I can't stay here any longer. My life was planned with Robbie. I don't know what I'll do..." Her voice trailed off as her eyes drifted off into the distance.

"Your mum and dad are going to need your support just as much as you need them."

Maria shook her head. "I can't. I can't stay here. They didn't know that Robbie and I were still seeing each other. It would destroy my parents."

Karen was just about to say something when Maria interrupted.

"I'm pregnant," she blurted out, fear etched in her eyes. "I'm carrying Robbie's baby. There's no way I can tell them."

Karen softened when she saw the despair on Maria's face. "I'm sure they'll understand. Something good can come of this horrible situation. A new life. A baby to keep your memories of Robbie alive."

Tears burst from Maria's eyes. "I won't be able to stay here. I know what my parents are like. They won't accept it. I'll have to leave."

"You don't know that yet. Let things settle for a while. Besides, where would you go?"

Maria shrugged. "I'm not sure. I've got friends in Malton. Perhaps I can stay there for a while."

Karen fished her car keys from her handbag. "I hope everything works out for you. Regardless of what your parents say, they will need you... and the baby."

HAVING LEFT THE RUTTERS, Karen drove to the Lawsons' farm, locked the car and walked past the farmhouse, giving it a brief and cursory glance before she headed to the fields that lay beyond it. The surrounding countryside was just as beautiful as Karen remembered. Cows mooed and grunted in a neighbouring field. The sound of a tractor carried on the light breeze as it made its way along twisting lanes somewhere in the distance. Crows cawed and clicked from the trees. Dried grass rustled beneath her feet.

Breathless, with a gleam of sweat on her face, Karen eventually stopped at the aged derelict farmhouse where the Lawson family had started life. She studied the old ruins and Edith Lawson's grave close by. The former farmhouse and the land surrounding it carried so much history. It had witnessed the circle of life from births to deaths.

Karen bowed her head in reflection and respect. "I hope I've got you the justice you all deserved."

PLEASE JOIN my reader's group for your free starter library:

www.jaynadal.com

CURRENT BOOK LIST

Hop over to my website for a current list of books:

www.jaynadal.com/current-books/

ABOUT THE AUTHOR

I've always had a strong passion for whodunnits, crime series and books. The more I immersed myself in it, the stronger the fascination grew.

In my spare time you'll find me in the gym, trying to squeeze in a read or enjoying walks in the forest...It's amazing what you think of when you give yourself some space.

Oh, and I'm an avid people-watcher. I just love to watch the interaction between people, their mannerisms, their way of expressing their thoughts...Weird I know.

I hope you enjoy the stories that I craft for you.

Author of:

The DI Scott Baker Crime Series

The DI Karen Heath Crime Series

The Thomas Cade PI Series